To [...]

I love [...] yr the best.

Twilight
of the
Lesser Gods

JOHN CALVIN HUGHES

JC

ISBN: 1467927104

ISBN: 9781467927109

To Britty

&

to Debbie

This book is a work of the imagination. All characters and events are entirely fictitious. No resemblance to real persons is intended or should be inferred. The cityscapes of Memphis, Mannheim, and Heidelberg are dream geographies.

CHAPTER ONE

Night sky burning pink, starless halogen glow of city lights, crooked trees black as split silk. Sgt. Jack Stuart stood in the shadow of a tree at the edge of the woods. Directly across from him on the back wall of the stockade was an obscured door, a door that only he knew, a door that opened into a low dank tunnel leading to a closet in his office in the middle of the building. The open ground between him and the door—twenty-five feet—was as brightly lit as an operating room. Only one guard tower had a sight line to the back wall. Stuart peered around the tree. He could not see the guard. Probably asleep on the floor.

To the north the yellow lights of Mannheim pushed up into the pink sky. Eastward the Neckar River slunk away toward Worms. Down the hill the guards' barracks were as brightly lighted as the city itself. *They never sleep.* Four guard platoons rotated the three watches. Stuart's platoon, First Platoon, was on its last night of three days off. Tomorrow they would go back on first shift, 0700 till 1500 hours. Then swing shift. Then graveyard and then three days off again. The constantly rotating schedule played hell with his sleeping, with everybody's sleep-ing. *It makes them crazy*, he thought. *It makes us crazy*.

Stuart stepped out into the pink light and crossed to the wall. As he felt along for the edge of the door, he remembered a dream he'd been having since he was a boy. In the dream he finds a door in his mother's house that he had never noticed be-fore, as if it had mysteriously been there the whole time. When he opens the door, he finds a huge suite of rooms, wonderful space right here under his nose, high-ceilinged, light-filled rooms that, though empty, fill him in his sleep with the com-fort of discovery and possession. It was one of his good dreams.

Stuart had not reported his discovery of the secret door into the stockade to the Sergeant Major. Nor to the Colonel, the commandant of the jail.

The door was sticky, but he managed to jimmy it open about a foot. He'd never actually used it since accidently discovering it over a year ago. Cleaning out the storage closet in his office one day, he found a panel on the back wall painted shut. Idle curiosity and a slow shift with nothing much to do led him to try prizing it open. When he did, he found a low narrow cor-ridor leading straight through the jail between the walls of the prisoner bays to a door on the back wall of the stockade. The next night, after his shift, he made his way through the woods behind the stockade to see if he could locate the door from the outside. These woods were strictly off limits, strung with con-certina wire and signs warning dire consequences for trespass-ing. The conventional wisdom said there were nuclear missile silos just beyond the tree line. But Stuart, who'd been in those same woods many times, had never found anything or anyone back there, certainly not missile silos. He had stared at the back wall a long time and finally thought he saw the faint line of a painted-over door edge. The next day he brought a couple of extra sets of fatigues to hang in the office closet to obscure the panel. But he had never had occasion to use the passage until tonight.

Inside the dank, low corridor, he turned on his flashlight and stooped through the puddly dark to his office. He was using the secret passage instead of coming in through the main gate because he didn't want the whole of Second Platoon, Sgt. Jones' platoon, to get wind of what was going on. Sgt. Kearns, Jones' assistant platoon leader, had called Stuart at the barracks. Stuart hadn't been able to understand everything Kearns was saying, but it was clear enough that the man was panicked and needed help. Stuart arrived in his closet, peeked out the door to make sure his office was empty, and called the front gate. Within seconds he could hear Kearns running down the hall. Kearns banged through the door, snapped to shivering attention, and saluted. "Sgt. Stuart, he's dead, the prisoner's dead, and I can't find Sgt. Jones, and you better come look cause I'm telling you he's dead, sir—"

"Wait," Stuart interrupted. "Don't call me sir. Who's dead? And, for God's sake, don't salute me. How long have you been in the Army? At ease, goddamn it, AT EASE! You're shaking like a leaf. Who's dead? Who in the hell is dead?"

Sgt. Kearns looked around at Stuart's office as if he'd never seen it before. "How did you get in? I was waiting at the front gate. Have you been here the whole time? I mean, uh—"

"KEARNS!"

"—prisoner, prisoner's dead in D Block, Watson, prisoner Watson, sir. Uh, Sergeant, I mean."

"Are you sure? Did you check his pulse? Are you goddamn sure he's dead?"

Kearns appeared to nod affirmatively, but he was shaking so hard Stuart couldn't be sure. Stuart picked up the phone and called Jernigan, the ranking NCO in the open prisoner bays. It was obvious that Kearns was not going to be of much use the rest of the night.

"Jerny, I want lock down, now. Yes, it's me. Lock down, you hear, now. Call the front gate. No, no, I'm inside. No, I don't know where Jones is. Look here, you lock it tight, hear me? Tight." Stuart's chest hurt. *Just the excitement, just the stress*, he told himself. Stuart pushed Kearns out of the way and ran down the north hall toward D Block. Two guards standing outside the A Block gate were so amazed to see Stuart—*running!*—they forgot to ask him where he was going or why he was in the jail when it wasn't his platoon's shift. And though they might have wanted to follow him, once the lock down horn sounded, nobody moved. Nobody *could* move. Nobody but Stuart.

It was deadly quiet in the stockade. D Block was the solitary confinement area, single cells for trouble makers, as well as for prisoners who needed to be segregated from the general population, the occasional officer or female or MP. Stuart approached the first of the three gates on the north hall. It was shut and locked. Private Jennifer Styles stood post. "Gate," Stuart panted in full stride, meaning open the gate. She did not move.

"Lock down, Sergeant."

"Who do think called the fucking lock down, Styles?" He had more to say, but Sgt. Jernigan came running full tilt down the hall from the other direction, slid to a skidding stop next to Styles, and bumped her out of the way. "Move, nitwit," he said, opening the gate with his own key, a big, flat brass key on a ring with many others.

He turned to Stuart at attention. "Sergeant, Prisoner Watson has killed hisself in D block. Hanged with his own sheet."

Stuart turned and strode quickly toward solitary, Jernigan hustling to keep up.

"Sheet? Sheet? Are you kidding me? Are you fucking kidding me? What did he secure it to? Where were the goddamn guards? Who's supposed to be on D block? Hey! You'd better get that fucking gate open before I get there or I'll—" But the second gate was open and the sentry pressed against the wall, out of the path of the two NCOs rushing toward the Close Confinement Area.

The eyes that peered at Stuart through the tiny peephole in the solid metal door to D block were scared, bloodshot, teary. Stuart thought he could read volumes into those eyes, if he had the time to think about it. The door swung open and Stuart stepped through. He stopped abruptly and pivoted toward the PFC who'd just closed the big heavy door, Private Milton. Milton was an acne-faced, border-line moron, according to Stuart's private IQ assessment. *Milton! Working close confinement! What was Sgt. Jones thinking?*

"Why the fuck is this gate open?" Yet another gate separated the big door from the cell area. "We've got a fucking lock down, Private. That means every fucking gate locked."

PFC Milton looked like he might faint any second now. He stammered, "Front gate called, Sgt. Stuart. Said you was coming back."

Stuart hrmphed. He stepped into the cell area and pulled the gate shut behind him. "Lock the goddamn thing now." Down the second row of cells he found Tony Jackson standing outside Cell Seven, arms crossed, shaking his head and chewing a toothpick. Jackson was one of Sgt. Jones' squad leaders, a tall, handsome black man about twenty-five, a longtime E-5, on the promotion list for over a year. Under Jones, Jackson would never get promoted. Still, he had the most smarts and the best character of anyone in Jones' platoon. Stuart had tried repeatedly to get Jackson transferred to First Platoon.

"This," Jackson said, moving the toothpick from one corner of his mouth to the other, "is a damn shame."

"Where's Jones?" Stuart stepped inside the tiny six by nine cell. The dead man appeared to be sitting on the floor leaning back against the wall of bars. A sheet was wrapped very tightly around his neck and the other end was tied around the waist-high bar running horizontally across the front of the cell. Stuart backed out and took a deep breath. Jackson nodded solemnly and looked over Stuart's shoulder toward the end of the corridor.

"Sgt. Jones isn't here," Jackson said. Stuart looked at him, but Jackson just shrugged. Jones was probably drunk in the gasthaus on the other side of the soccer field. Jackson said, "I sent Woods and the rest up to the chaplain's office as soon as I got here. Just to get them out of the way."

Goddamn it, Stuart thought. *Jones assigned Woods to D block! What was he trying to do?*

He tried to slow his breathing, but his chest was tight and his legs felt weak. He leaned against the wall and closed his eyes. After a minute Jackson asked if he was okay.

Stuart ignored him and went back into the cell and knelt in front of the dead man. Watson. *Jesus Christ.* A bad-attitude punk from New Jersey or some other east coast shithole who'd never adjusted to the Army. Probably should have fallen out in Basic Training, but somehow got through, got assigned to Germany, a string of Article 15's, loss of pay several times, finally court-martialed for stealing. Dumbass stole a boom box from a soldier in his own barracks. Set the damn thing on top of his locker like nobody'd notice. Got three years in Leavenworth and a dishonorable discharge. Just stopping here long enough to do the paperwork before flying back to the world. Couldn't even stay out of trouble in here. Stuart had had to throw him into the box himself first day, little shit had cussed him out twice.

Stuart sighed. "Gloves, sergeant." Jackson opened his mouth to say something, then thought better of it, came to attention, and marched off toward the office. *Better to go by the book now*, Stuart thought. *He's got his ideas, I damn sure got mine.*

When he'd pulled on the latex gloves, he told Jackson to cancel the lock down, call the Criminal Investigation Division, and go to the barracks to get his Polaroid. He handed Jackson his room key. "I'll call the CO and the Colonel. Don't say anything. To anybody." Jackson frowned as if to say that went without saying. But Stuart just shook his head and repeated, "Not to anybody."

CHAPTER TWO

1 May 1977, 0700 hours
Coleman Kaserne
Mannheim, Germany

Stuart didn't tell him to stay. Neither did Kearns, so as soon as the shift ended Carl Woods banged out the front gate of the stockade and headed for the gasthaus beyond the soccer field which lay just outside the fence around the base, or the *kaserne* as folks called it. The gate from the soccer field onto the kaserne was unguarded since it was in plain sight of two of the guard towers at the biggest U.S. Army stockade in Europe. It stayed unlocked all day and into the evening. The guards on the graveyard shift would usually lock it around midnight, so most of the soldiers coming back from the gasthaus would have to walk all the way around to the front entrance of the kaserne to get back to their barracks. Or else they'd try to climb over some unpatrolled stretch of the fence. He had climbed that fence himself several times himself back when he was living in the barracks, before his wife, Lil, came over. Not that he'd *had* to climb, mind you. If you were a guard from the jail, one of the sentries would walk over from the stockade and unlock the gate for you. No, when he'd climbed the fence, he had climbed it for the absolute and pure hell of it.

Though it was only seven in the morning, he was going to get as drunk as Cooter Brown. He followed a group of guards from his platoon across the sunny soccer field. The sky was painfully bright blue, not a cloud in sight. Beyond the soccer field and the gasthaus, past the houses of this suburb of Mannheim, tall dark pine trees loomed up out of the woods that the Germans let stand right inside the city limits. He stopped just outside the entrance to the gasthaus and looked at the building's facade. It looked like something out of a fairy tale. Like a gingerbread house or some shit. Certainly like nothing he had ever seen back in Arkansas.

Inside, the large room was very bright and cheerful, some Germans drinking coffee and eating rolls for breakfast, some guards ordering beers and getting bad looks from the German customers. Not many locals came here anymore, and especially not at night when the whole kaserne was off duty. Soldiers from every company on base drank here, but most of the regular business came from the 77th MP Detachment, whose members walked over from the stockade after shift or came straight from supper at the mess hall and spent the evening drinking. The gasthaus being so close to the jail and all, it had become kind of a tradition and a home court situation with the guards and even with some of the dick wads from the 77th's administrative platoon.

A couple of guards from his platoon called to him to come over, but he waved them off and sat near the window, drinking schnapps and beer. He felt like shit. He didn't trust any of the other guards. Since his enlistment, the main most thing he'd learned was that you can't make friends among soldiers. Not real friends anyway. They're not trustworthy. To a man, they're back stabbers. Also they're stupid. The all volunteer Army was the stupidest idea ever come up with and mainly because you had to be stupid to join the Army. He'd himself been just that stupid.

Some of the guards had ordered and were drinking wine and coke. *Ugh.* Most of them were so young they didn't really know how to drink. Probably never had a drink before. And even if they'd drunk some beer back home, they damn sure hadn't had anything like this German beer. It was strong as hell and bitter as a weed. These wet dicks needed something else, something that tasted sweet. And since the Germans didn't have no Boone's Farm Apple, these boys drank white wine cut with co-cola. They were talking in loud voices about the asses they'd kicked, the pussy they'd fucked, and the cons they'd whipped. Woods shook his head. He doubted many of them had had any pussy except off the whores on P Street, and they damn sure didn't know anything about cons.

But he knew. Nobody understood that scum the way he did. He knew them inside and out. And now that maggot Watson was dead. Well, Stuart would handle that. Whatever Stuart suspected, whatever he thought might have happened, hell, whatever he *knew as God's truth*, Stuart would fix it so that no heat ever came down. Stuart hated Woods' guts, but he couldn't prove anything. For that matter, Stuart wouldn't even try to prove anything. He never let the shit come down on the guards. Unless they were stupid enough to get caught at something red-handed. No, Stuart would take care of it. That much he knew.

An hour later when Woods stood up, he nearly fell over the next table. Staggering into the restroom, standing there, pissing against the wall, he thought about the Germans. *Fucking Germans.* Why even bother to put in a goddamn bathroom if you weren't going to put in a goddamn toilet or urinal, if you were just going to have to piss on the wall anyway? What in the hell were they thinking? You could piss against a wall outside just as well. Hell, there's already a wall outside. For that god-damn matter you could piss against a tree, or a car, or you could piss on the ground. Or on your shoes, if you're drunk enough. And he was just about drunk enough.

He stumbled outside to get some air and stood sucking in deep cold lungfuls, staring back across the soccer field at the stockade. It was like a huge gray box sitting back against the woods. He started across the field toward the gate, but worried he might run into Stuart. No telling how long the old fucker'd have to stay at the jail today, talking his way out of it, covering his ass. Covering Woods' ass. So he turned and followed the fence line down into the trees and found a spot where the concertina wire was smashed down from people climbing it, and he pulled himself up on top and tried to swing his legs over. He lost his balance. His pants leg caught on the wire, and he fell over onto the hard ground. The fall knocked the wind out of him, and then when he could breathe again, he threw up a couple of steins of beer. Too drunk to get home. He'd never make it. First of all, he would have to figure out the right bus going his way, try not fall asleep and end up in Bremerhaven or some fucking place. He might could make it to the barracks if the world would stop spinning for a minute, but he'd never make it all the way back to Donner strasse street, to his tiny apartment, to Lil. He pulled himself up and leaned back against a skinny pine, just inside the fence. The sun was shining down through the pine needles. He felt warm and safe, out of the wind. He could probably stay out here all day and not get caught. But, shit, if he could just make the barracks, he could sleep on the couch in the dayroom. Nobody'd think nothing of it. He closed his eyes.

———

Two years ago back in Arkansas he'd come home and told her he'd gotten fired. They'd been married less than a month. Lil just stood there staring at him. She didn't understand what that meant, he thought. She just looked scared. Course, she'd looked scared since the first time he saw her. She said nothing. He took the last beer from the icebox and sat out on the porch in the blinding heat. It was the middle of the day in the middle of summer in the middle of Arkansas. He would have sent her to the store for more beer, but they wouldn't sell it to her since she was too young. Too hot to walk down there himself.

But he *had* walked down there and got *two* six packs and spent the afternoon rocking on the porch, hollering at Lil to bring him beers and waiting on some breeze to stir or some little hint of rain. Every once in a while a pickup or car would drive down the road and kick up the red dust and push hot red air up over him, onto his face. Late in the afternoon, black thunderheads humped over the horizon and darkened the sky and sucked all the color out of the world. In a few minutes it began to rain, a little at first, but then fast and hard. So loud on the tin roof of the porch that it was impossible to hear anything else. The wind gusted and blew the rain sideways up onto the porch, driving him inside.

In the little house it was dark and drafty and jumpy around the edges of things and ragged in the corners of the room. He went around and shut all the windows. It was stifling in the house. Then he went into the kitchen where Lil was washing the dishes.

She had been in the kitchen washing dishes in front of the open window, the curtain blowing in her face, falling and whipping up again. A crack of thunder made her jump. When she turned around and saw him, she started again, like he was the thunder himself.

"Girl, you can't wash no dishes in a thunderstorm." She didn't say anything, just stood with her wet, soapy hands held out limply before her. He was plainly drunk, a sly grin on his puffy, boyish face. He stood there swaying slightly, then pulled his sweat-soaked T shirt over his head and dropped it *splat* on the floor. She knew what that meant. *God, in this heat!* She turned back to the sink and put her hands into the gritty gray water. He came up behind her and kissed her neck, rubbed his strong hands on her belly and breasts, smelling like sweat and beer. He leaned against her and pushed her hard against the sink, mashing her stomach and legs. He rocked slowly against her and bent her farther and farther over until her face was nearly in the dishwater. Then he stood up straight and pulled her by the hand into the bedroom.

The coming storm and yellow window shades gave the room a sickly color. He'd closed the windows. The room, oh the room was unbearably hot. They had bought the place furnished, since neither of them had anything really when they got married, and still now there was only a bed and a dresser in the room. There had been a buckled and sun-faded print in a dusty frame up on the wall, the only decoration in the whole place, a picture of two women, one playing the piano, both of them at the foot of a winding staircase, but she had taken it down and stuck it in the back of a closet. It was too tacky. Better a bare wall.

She slipped the straps of her pink sundress off her shoulders and let it drop to the floor. He wanted it on the floor, she knew. She had tried to hang it up before, but he said drop it on the floor, so she always dropped it on the floor, whatever it was, shorts, T shirt, nightgown, right on the floor. He always stepped on whatever clothes it was. He didn't really make a point of it, but still always stepped on them just the same. Now she sat in her panties on the edge of the bed and watched him. And now he'd stripped naked and was sitting on the floor with his back to her, digging dirty clothes out of the big black garbage bag she carried them to the laudrymat in. She knew what he was looking for. Sweat socks. Dirty sweat socks, preferably some he'd worked in recently. To tie her hands behind her back and gag her. This was the way he'd taught her to make love, and since she'd been with no other man before, had never been made love to by any other than this crazy man, she had no reason to doubt it was the proper way, the only way. Sometimes he put a pillowcase over her head. *God*. She hoped he wouldn't. She hated that. Even the dirty sock in her mouth didn't bother her as much as that.

She did like to look at him, though, at his nakedness. He was big and muscled up as a horse. His hair was shiny black and she liked it when he was just out of the shower and had his hair all slicked back. It was otherwise a bad haircut, long and uneven and shapeless, falling down around his fat baby face. But he liked to walk around the house naked just after a shower, hair all slicked back, arm muscles bulging like big cathead biscuits, and though she'd never seen any other man's thing for comparison, she believed his was a pretty one, just a little dauber when he was walking around, but big and trembly when the time was right. She wished she enjoyed doing this more. Or even at all. Truth be told, it wasn't even a little fun. She tried to avoid it however she could, gave any excuse she could think of: tired, bleeding, already asleep, not tired enough to go to bed. Whatever it took. Now he found what he was looking for and threw the socks onto the bed. He stood up and kicked the other dirty clothes into the corner of the room.

Sweat was running in little rivers down his body. She wanted to reach up and touch him, especially his arms where the muscles bunched up, and kiss him on his hard belly, maybe his nipples.

But that kinda stuff had never come up in their lovemaking. What she wanted. What she wanted was pretty clearly not the point. Now she knew what to do. She lay back on the bed and was very still. He rolled her onto her stomach and pulled her arms back. With a sweat sock, he tied them together at the wrist, then brushed her long brown hair aside and kissed the pale freckles dusted across her white shoulders and back like stars. He kissed her all the way down to her panties, and then tugged them down over her thighs and kissed her butt cheeks, kneading the big muscles there so hard she'd be sore the next day. He ran his tongue up and down the crack, prodding the tight button of her hole. He liked her behind, liked to tease and torment it, though he never tried to get inside her that way. When he was satisfied with this, he pulled her panties all the way off and rolled her over to face him.

She knew her breasts were small, but she hoped they might still grow a bit someday. Not that it would matter to him because he didn't seem to care about them anyway, never really touched or kissed them. She opened her mouth as wide as she could, and he stuffed in a sock and pulled her legs apart. Kneeling above her, he licked his finger and spread the spittle all over the head of his thing. He did this over and over until it was glistening and big and full to bursting. Then he leaned over and put it inside her.

She figured it was probably a good thing she *was* tied up the first time he did it to her. He entered so quickly it always hurt, but that first time it hurt so badly she'd moaned in her gag and cried. Now it only hurt at first. Usually it took him a pretty good while to get done. He rocked on top of her for what seemed like hours, though it was probably only like twenty or thirty minutes. Sometimes, though, after he'd been at it a while, he couldn't do what he wanted, couldn't "get there," he said. Then he would roll her over and untie her quick and go sit in the living room in the dark and grunt and growl like he was hurt, and sometimes cry. She had felt sorry for him, then, wondered what was wrong. She figured it couldn't be anything she was doing because, well, she wasn't really *doing* anything.

Sometimes she thought maybe she could "get there" if she could just move around a little better. She knew what it was and had done it to herself before, taught by her first cousin Cathy, a fat, pug-nosed little brat with a brown Prince Valiant haircut from Little Rock. Cathy could "get there" like nobody's business and she liked to a lot. Lil hadn't done that to herself during the month she'd been married to Carl because she wasn't real sure whether he would want her to or not. For that matter, she didn't know if she was supposed to be doing it at all, or if she was even supposed to know how to do it.

But tonight Carl finished in no time. Let out a big yell and made a crazy face, and then got up and tied her feet together. This was something new. Usually he untied her hands after he caught his breath. Now he tied her feet and left the room. And she needed to pee. He surely knew that. But she couldn't get up and go now. All she could do was just lay there, dripping his seed, aching in her shoulders, needing the bathroom.

Carl Woods hunched forward on the couch. The living room was awash in blue light from the soundless TV, the patterns of light bouncing on the walls and on his face. The house was utterly quiet. He wanted quiet now. Once he heard Lil trying to call out and struggling to get loose. If he untied her now, she'd be in the kitchen or the bathroom, talking to herself, running the water, banging pots or something. So he'd left her tied up. He needed it quiet. She wouldn't mind too much, he thought.

His face felt numb. He felt paralyzed, mouth open, staring a thousand yards off into empty space. He was thinking about Mr. Hardigan, his boss. His ex-boss. Today he'd told Carl his work was not up to standards. Not up to standards. Not punctual. Poor attitude. *It's you, Mr. Hardigan, who has the poor attitude. I have troubles at home that you have no idea how bad they are. I've tried my dead level best and nothing's never good enough for you.* That's what he should have said. That was the bitch of it. He could always think later what he should have said then. Instead he just pushed Hardigan down, called him a bastard, and left. And now he was fired. Now he was out of work.

The TV light flickered in the deep silence. All the windows were still shut. The storm had passed, and the twilight was quiet and still. Without the windows open to let in the evening cool, the house was like an oven. *It's a quiet hot*, he thought. Earlier he had pictured several scenes of Hardigan's death, all variations on the same theme, but he was through thinking about that now. Now his mind was empty, the house still. He leaned back on the couch and stared at the ceiling, turned his head and looked at the wall, the crummy peeling wallpaper, the crummy little house. He sat still, paralyzed, frozen and burning in this little oven of a house. He listened to the nothing. He listened as hard as he could to the nothing. He wondered how silence could be so loud. Then it happened.

The icebox motor kicked on. He listened to the icebox hum with the same concentration that he had been listening to the nothing. He listened and listened, and he thought that under the noise of the icebox, or maybe it was behind the noise of the icebox, he thought that he could hear voices. Or were they *inside* the noise of the icebox? Somewhere back in there. Or now he thought maybe it was just one voice, he couldn't be sure. He strained to hear what they were saying. He closed his eyes and leaned forward. It sounded like they were yelling, screaming to be heard over the rushing machine sound of the icebox. But real faint. He thought he was just on the verge of making out some of the words they were saying when the motor abruptly shut off and plunged the house back into silence. The quiet hissed like a snake around him.

Then something shifted at the edge of his vision. An old faded green wingback chair stood in the corner of the room. It was so hot in the room he thought he would explode. His face was numb, burning, he couldn't move. He could only stare at the crumbling chair. It seemed to shimmer like a heat mirage in the flickering light. Then the chair nudged forward an inch. And then. And then. A hand slowly crawled, finger by finger, over the back of the chair. Then. The voice.

The voice from behind the chair choked him, like dirt in his throat, hit him in the chest, hot and cold and deep, and grabbed him in the stomach and squeezed. When the thing crept out from behind the chair, tiny old-fashioned spectacles, thick mustache, stooped, squinting, moss and dirt hanging on its collar, from its pockets, it spoke. Woods recoiled, every muscle spasmed, mouth wide open in a mute, nightmare scream. And though every part of the thing reeked of the rot, of the grave, dead, dead, dead, he could stand its presence, its *being there*, but not the voice. Anything but the voice. He could understand none of the words but knew their meaning. Woods squeezed his eyes shut, but the voice sawed into him and carved him inside. It felt like a huge hand had hold of his balls and was squeezing, slowly, harder and harder. He lay back on the couch. *If it doesn't kill me, it'll make me, oh god, oh god, let go!* Its sour breath.

———

Woods really came fully to himself only after he'd killed the first dog. The recoil of the shotgun and the concussion shook him fully awake. The hound—Woods' best—stupid fool dog, had just walked right up and taken it between the eyes. The other two scurried to the far corner of the pen. It took him a few minutes to corner and kill them.

Lil eased her stiff limbs slowly into the tub and lay back in the milky-white water, closing her eyes and sighing. She slid down into the water until it reached her mouth. Drawing in a little of the water, she made a sputtering sound like a motorboat. The water tasted brackish and soapy.

She'd heard the shots still lying on the bed, but when he came in and untied her, she didn't ask him what he'd been shooting at. Later he came into the bathroom and sat on the floor next to the tub. She sat up and hugged her knees, wondering *what now*? He was looking at the floor, trying to say something. There were tiny flecks of blood on the front of his blue work shirt. She had a bad moment, thinking he was going to leave her. Her stomach squeezed up tight like a closed fist and she nearly cried. Finally he looked up.

"I've decided to join the Army. I don't think I can find another job around here."

"What about me? Are you gonna leave me here?"

"I guess I'll have to for a while." She began to cry, and he said, "It won't be for long, maybe a couple of months, I don't know, but then you'll come with me wherever they send me, I promise."

He stood up and looked down at her. She settled back down into the water. He stepped into the tub in his shoes and all his clothes and hunkered down over her. "It's going to be okay, I swear." He leaned forward and lay down on top of her, pushing her down, his clothes soaking up the bath water, splashing some of it out onto the floor. He was so big and heavy she knew he could drown her easily if he took a mind to, could even do it accidently. With one hand she reached around him and held onto his back, grabbing the side of the tub with the other, straining to keep her head above water.

Carl had been in the Army two years when he killed that maggot Watson. He'd wanted to be an MP, but for some damn reason the Army'd held him out, made him become a stockade guard instead. He'd been turned down at the police academy in Little Rock too, the year before he came into the Army. He wanted to be a cop, always had. Well, for five years anyway, ever since he'd nearly gotten caught breaking into the liquor store at Farley Corners. An Arkansas highway patrolman had questioned him, but nothing ever came of it. He'd gotten away with fifty-seven dollars and three fifths of Black Jack. Took four, dropped one running. But he never forgot that patrolman, big bastard, shiny bloused boots, starched uniform, Smokey the Bear hat, and those mirrored sunglasses, just like something out of the movies. And now sometimes at formation, with Sgt. Jones looking for the Supernumero—the guard who looked the best, who would be released from duty for looking so good—he felt like that, like that patrolman, his uniform crisp, as hard as Lil could starch it, his back straight, eyes ahead. Fuck it, though. Jones never picked him. Sent some other son of a bitch home, free shift off just for looking good, standing tall. Bullshit. Fuck Jones, the horse's ass bastard.

The rain woke Woods up. For a second he thought he was back in Arkansas, sleeping out in the trees behind his house. It was almost full dark. He climbed back over the fence and headed toward the gasthaus, toward the bus stop there. Twenty minutes later, the right bus came and he climbed on without a ticket and fell into a seat in the back. The bus veered north through the rain toward downtown Mannheim. Carl didn't know any of the names of the streets except his own. He was sorry now he'd brought Lil to Germany after all. He should have just sent her back to her daddy and been done with it. Stay here alone. Then he could live in the barracks. That's where everything was, everything worth doing or talking about, decent television, Coke machines, people who speak fucking English. Other guards, especially the few who really understood what the jail was all about. He was headed now for his apartment on Donner strasse street. He'd have to walk three blocks from the bus stop. He hated Germany. And the Germans, stuck-up bastards, hating his guts, hating all Americans. Never mind that the Americans were here to keep the fucking Russians out of the Fulda Pass, out of their back-goddamn-yards, for *them*, goddamn Germans, not anything in it for America. Never mind he was paying twice the rent of the other people in the building, the *German* tenants, and paying the whole electric bill for all three apartments in his building. Oh, he knew that. Someday he'd get that landlord, Herr Weiss. The right Herr-fucking-Weiss would get his. Never mind that the one garbage can for the whole apartment building wouldn't even hold his and Lil's trash for the week much less two other families' too and that twice a week he had to carry his garbage all the way to Coleman-fucking-kaserne to dump it, carry it on the damn bus like it was a suitcase or something and not a stinking bag of trash. Not that anyone could smell it over the stinking Germans. Fuckers never bathed.

The bus deposited him in front of a bakery, and he spat at the door. Once he'd tried to buy some cake or donuts to take to the jail, but the people pretended not to know what he was saying and didn't even try to understand when he pointed at what he wanted. He cussed them out but good and left and never went back. Two blocks on this street and then turn on Donner strasse. He was wet and his stomach still hurt from puking. Streetlights bounced back pink off the cloud cover. He passed Herr Weiss' house. *Someday for that bastard*, he thought.

Lil had to be lonely, a young girl so far from her family, so far from anyone who spoke good English or even had any manners. When Lil first got here and he moved out of the barracks, some of the guys came over a couple of times, drank some beer, talked with Lil and him, listened to some music, but gradually they stopped coming over. He could understand why. There was nothing to do. You couldn't just raise hell out on the economy among the proper Germans the way you could in the barracks. If you raised your voice after ten, people above and below pounded and yelled at you. So he and Lil just sat around and listened to music. And she read. There was no TV. Well, there was German TV, that didn't make a goddamn bit of sense, so they stopped watching. He'd never been able to get his television to pick up the Armed Forces Network station from Frankfurt with all the American reruns the way you could at the barracks in the dayroom.

He'd shown her one day how to get to Coleman kaserne on the bus, how to show her ID to the guard and get to the library from the front gate. So she went and she read. He supposed she read all day. She damn sure read all night. Once she'd asked him if she could apply for a job at the PX or the bowling alley on the kaserne. *A lot of dependents worked there*, she said. But he told her no, and that was the end of it. He didn't tell her that he didn't want her around soldiers all day. She was young, would talk to anybody, liable to believe any lie those pussy hounds told her. He knew how GIs acted. Anything with a slit. Literally anything. The ugliest woman in the world, put her on or near an Army post and she'll get chased like a white-tail deer. Didn't matter, soldiers wanted pussy, period. Ugly, don't take 'em nowhere. Can't talk, don't talk to 'em, can't walk, don't walk 'em nowhere. Eight to eighty, blind, crippled or crazy. Be damned if he was gonna have Lil there eight hours a day, five, six days a week. So she read.

The building they lived in was indistinguishable from the others on the block except that theirs was on the corner. Square building, square windows, like living in a box. New though. Nothing in the whole city of Mannheim was over thirty years old, smashed completely flat by American bombers in World War Two. He stood for a minute on the opposite corner looking up at the second story window, the kitchen window. He saw a shadow pass, her moving around, cooking or something. Somebody from the attic apartment stepped into the staircase and turned on the light. He could see the shape of the person coming down the stairs, twisted and deformed by the glass bricks that the wall had been built out of. He stepped back into the bushes that grew tall around the giant bomb shelter that sat on that corner, undisturbed, he imagined, since the last war. A man came out of the stairwell door and walked quickly off toward the bus stop, leaning against the rising wind. Carl watched his figure slowly disappear and then looked again at the building where he lived. His home. In a couple of minutes the light in the stairwell turned itself off.

CHAPTER THREE

13 July 1977, 0100 hours
Autobahn A61
Approaching Mannheim, Germany

After the third stop, only six soldiers remained on the bus. Fifty-one had boarded in Frankfurt. Culp moved up from the back and took a window seat near the middle. Four PFCs were jabbering back there, trying to scare up a card game. One guy sat up front looking over the driver's shoulder into the glare of headlights on the wet autobahn. It was pitch black outside— they were away from any city. Culp had arrived in country only today and had no idea where he was or even whether he was headed north or south.

All the soldiers on the bus had arrived in country that day. A couple of the guys in the back had been on the plane from South Carolina with Culp. It had been a sort of military slash civilian flight, with regular stewardesses, but no drinks. Soldiers and their families who'd never been farther than fifty miles from home going to Europe. The cabin had been hot and stuffy and somebody's kid cried a lot. An eleven-hour trip, utterly sleepless for Culp, followed by a welcome to Germany from some Air Force officer and an all-day wait in crummy plastic airport chairs. Everybody waiting for duty station assignments. An Air Force sergeant had marched over at one point to talk to the new arrivals about living and working in Germany. "This block of instruction is designed to help orientate you to some of the important cultural differences between yourselves and the local German natives of this country." The whole speech had taken about ten minutes. All Culp remembered was the sergeant saying not to jaywalk because the Germans would run you over. "They don't drive like us," he'd said, "and eventually neither will you."

For some reason, probably exhaustion, surely fear, the phrase "person, place, or thing" kept running through his mind during his orientation. Under stress, Culp always got one stupid phrase stuck in his head. Usually some song lyric. Maybe having to face a nation of non-English speakers was forcing him take babbling refuge inside the rules of grammar. Late in the afternoon he'd heard his name blared over the loud speaker and saw a soldier at the far end of the terminal waving him over. He click-clocked across the shining floor toward the counter. "Orders," the soldier said, and Culp handed over a copy. He had sixty more copies with him. "Go through this door to the Destination Room, see Specialist Boyer." *Person, place, or thing*, Culp thought.

The Destination Room was a gymnasium-sized space honeycombed by chest-high dividers into little nests of paperwork. In one of the cubicles Specialist Boyer was standing up so Culp could find him. He had a cup of coffee in one hand, a cigarette in the other, and a phone receiver jammed up between his shoulder and his ear. Culp made his way over and sat down. Boyer was a typical Army clerk, bleary eyes, rumpled Class A uniform, world-weary attitude. He cursed and hung up the phone, then threw the short unfiltered butt onto the grimy linoleum and stomped it with a squinty-eyed viciousness, grinding it down as if it might try to crawl away like some bug.

"Where would you like to be assigned? Your wish list?" He thumbed through Culp's 201 file and orders.

Wha? Culp was not remotely prepared for this question. Someone should have told him he might have such a choice. It was too overwhelming. Whatever he said now could, and probably would, affect his next two years in ways he could never imagine. A word now and the cone of future possibilities would narrow into unpredictable and almost certainly terrible configurations. *Jesus*, he thought. San Antonio to South Carolina to Frankfurt. He was tired. He was scared. Boyer stared at him. Culp shrugged helplessly.

Boyer sighed. He leaned back in his chair and looked into his coffee cup. "I hate drinking out of Styrofoam." He drank off the dregs and made a face.

Culp said, "Can't you just bring a cup from home? I mean, and leave it in your desk?"

Specialist Boyer leaned forward and lowered his voice. "Tried it. Stolen. Three times."

"How could somebody, I mean, why would somebody even *want*—?"

"What pisses me is that other people here have cups. Leave them right out on their desks. Nobody bothers them. Tell you the truth, I don't think anybody wants my cup. No. I think it's personal."

Culp said, "That's just crazy."

"You said it. I just—wait. You mean it's crazy to steal my cups or I'm crazy to think it's personal?"

"The first," Culp said.

"Okay. Yeah. Crazy. So what's your first choice of duty station?"

"I mean, I don't know. I just got here. This place looks okay. How about here, in Frankfurt, I mean?"

"What the hell's a 91 Golf–Behavioral Science Specialist?"

Culp sighed. "It's like a counselor. You know, like the guys who work at Mental Hygiene?"

"Never been. Look. Frankfurt's choice duty, old son. You can't just walk in and say 'Frankfurt', you know?" He leaned back in his chair and eyed Culp. "You know anybody? Got any friends here in Frankfurt?"

Culp didn't. Boyer dug down into the morass of paper covering his desk and finally came up with Culp's fate. The closest duty station with a request for a 91G was Mannheim. He typed up new orders for Culp, assigning him to the 42nd MP Group (Customs) at Drexel kaserne in Mannheim. Culp stared at the words a long time waiting for the bus. What is Drexel kaserne? Where is Mannheim? What would a customs group want with a counselor?

A counselor. Culp shuddered at the thought that he would be expected to "counsel" anybody. If his training as a counselor indicated anything about how the rest of the Army was trained, the Army was in trouble. If those guys firing nuclear missiles didn't know anything more about missiles than Culp knew about the human psyche, there was a good chance they would blow themselves and the whole goddamn world up. His training at Ft. Sam Houston was pretty simple: college freshman-level Psychology, Sociology, and Social Work; interviewing techniques; and survey of social resources. Ten weeks. The attrition rate was 65% after the first test. Of the forty enlisted men and women who started the course, twelve finished. The ones who'd washed out were pushed off into more strenuous occupations in the infantry, artillery, or ground support units. And, in fact, many of those poor bastards had only reenlisted to get into the Behavioral Science school. Now they were stuck with another hitch, three, four years for most, back in the same old jobs as before, or worse. Most Army schools you could just take the course again and eventually become what it was you wanted to be, but not this one. This was an exception, and Culp could see why now. The Behavioral Science instructors knew they couldn't make dumbass grunts into counselors in ten weeks, so they simply made the course so hard that only the smartest or most hard-working went out into the field. Or those like Culp who'd had a couple of years of college.

After basic training, the Behavioral Science school at Ft. Sam Houston seemed like a dream. Very slack, by military standards. The whole base was entirely dedicated to training the Army's medical personnel. No one wore fatigues. It was Class A khakis every day. No guns, no runs, no PT, no pushups, no screaming drill sergeants. Just keep the barracks clean and go to class. It was easy. Not that different from college really. Culp hadn't gained much muscle tone in Basic despite the hard training. What little he did have he quickly lost at Ft. Sam. The food was better, the regimen relaxing. Culp had put on some pounds there. He was squeezed into his uniform now.

Somewhere up ahead in the distance the lights of a city shimmered. Would that be his city? Would he even be stationed in a city? Hell, the 42nd MPs could be in the middle of nowhere. Or, no, on some border. Customs, right? And for that matter, why wasn't the customs group in Frankfurt? That's where incoming troops arrived. And what in the world could they want with him? Trying to imagine the different MP and customs scenarios in which he might play a role, he fell into an unexpected and fitful sleep.

He woke with a start from a horrible dream of basic training. It was still night, but the bus was no longer on the autobahn. Huge dark buildings floated by as close as the window. The streets were empty. Clean and empty.

His watch was still on South Carolina time. He stood up and made his way unsteadily to the front of the bus. "What time is it? Where are we?"

"Figured I'd have to wake you up, soldier. You's snoring like a buzz saw. This'll be your stop. Mannheim." The bus driver pointed up ahead into the glare. "Gotta cross to the north side of town to drop you off."

Twenty minutes later the driver turned sharply into a narrow gate and was waved through by the sentries. "Drexel kaserne. Kaserne, boy. That's German for Army base. And I guess I'll be dropping you right here."

They stopped before one of the indistinguishable buildings, and the driver got out to open the luggage door. Culp pulled his duffel bag and suitcase out and dropped them on the ground. The driver turned and climbed onto the bus without another word. Culp stood breathing the fumes from the departing bus as long as they lasted. In front of the next building, several jeeps with MP insignia and blue lights were dressed in razor sharp lines like troops. Culp felt a distinct urge to run. Fight or flight. But there was no threat and no place to run. He was lost. Standing in front of his new unit, his first unit really, the slow beginning of the long, stretched out end of his Army tour, and he was as lost as he could be. Only two years to go. In all his life he had never felt this. He had felt fear plenty, and he had felt lost. But he had never felt there were no options. There were always options. That was the trouble with life, too many choices. Now he had none. No, not none—one. That door, the one to the 42nd MP Group. He could walk through that door or he could—what? Go back out the gate into Mannheim?

Though it was a nice cool night, he was sweating. Nevertheless, he buttoned up his jacket and straightened his cap. He shouldered his duffel bag the best he could and dragged the suitcase behind him. The door led into the orderly room. A sleepy corporal nearly broke his neck trying to get up off the couch, not expecting anyone that time of night and not knowing whether Culp might be some inspecting general. Culp dropped his gear and stood perfectly at attention. He snapped a salute and bellowed, "Private Culp, reporting for duty, SIR!" He tried to hold his stomach in.

The corporal, fully awake now, fell back onto the couch and rubbed his eyes. He looked up at Culp who was trembling with rigidity and still holding the salute. "Relax, man, this ain't Basic and I damn sure ain't no officer." Culp slowly dropped the salute and looked around. Green metal filing cabinets, gray desks, old typewriters. The floor was spotless, buffed to a high gloss. "Cupacoffee?" the corporal said. Culp shook his head. "Well, I'm going to have one. Sit down, take a load off. Long ride? Yeah, I guess so. Really only about an hour and a half to Frankfurt, as the crow flies, but I guess you dropped a lot of passengers twixt here and there, huh?" Culp nodded. The corporal splashed coffee into a filthy cup and said, "Yeah, lots of new meat for the old sausage grinder, huh?"

Sausage grinder? *What the hell is this guy talking about*, Culp thought. The corporal was blowing steam off his coffee and sniffing the steamy aroma. A large purple birthmark covered his left cheek. "Are you the CQ?" Culp asked.

"Assistant. Sergeant Wright, he's the CQ. He's asleep in the back there. Shit, I hate to wake him up." He looked over his shoulder and whispered, "A real sombitch, you know?" Sure, Culp knew. The Army breeds sons of bitches. Hell, if you weren't a son of a bitch, you were the rare, rare exception.

The corporal knocked on a door that Culp thought might have led to a closet. He didn't go into the room, but stuck his head in and said something in a low voice. When he came back, he nodded at Culp and sat down at a desk with his coffee and began reading a copy of *Stars and Stripes* as if that's what he'd been doing it all night, instead of sleeping on the couch. A few minutes later the CQ emerged.

Sergeant Wright was a tall, heavy E-6 with military issue glasses and a brown walrus mustache. He was too old to be just a staff sergeant, and he looked tired, but, thankfully, he didn't give Culp any shit. He took five copies of Culp's orders and told him to report to the first sergeant in the morning. Then he told the corporal to take Culp to the transient room where he could spend the rest of the night. "And get your ass back quick," Wright said. The corporal rolled his eyes at Culp.

The transient room was a standard barracks room. Culp could have been back at Ft. Sam. Four lockers, two double bunks, one trashcan. But looking out the window was another story. Nothing about Drexel kaserne looked anything like any Army post he had ever seen. The buildings were so—*German* or something. They were too tall, too wide, too old-world. Inside, yes, military all the way, but outside looked like a travel poster, at least what he could see of it by the pink halogen lights. Typically Army, the room smelled of strong detergent and dirty mops. Culp climbed up onto one of the top bunks and lay down in his clothes. He cried for just a minute and hated himself for it, but then felt better.

He must have dozed because the sound of the door shutting woke him. At first he thought he was dreaming. *The door hadn't opened, had it?* Though he was lying on his side facing the wall, he could tell the door was shut because it was dark in the room, and the hallway lights would brighten things considerably if the door were open. He lay still, listening to the night sounds of the barracks. Then he heard a shoe scrape on the floor. Fear tensed every muscle in him so tightly he thought he might cry out. A deep voice grumbled out of the dark.

"It's a jab, man. A-fucking-firmative. That cherry's got the dime, the line, and the life of crime." Another voice snorted assent.

Culp rolled over very slowly and looked at the two men sitting on the wide window sill. The window was open, swung out on hinges like a door. Culp had never seen a window like it. The men were just silhouettes. One of them was big, really big. The deep voice. Could probably kill Culp with his bare hands. The other was small and thin and holding a pipe. He flicked a lighter and illuminated their faces for a moment. Black men. The little man passed the pipe to the big man.

Culp recognized the smell. Hash. He had smoked a lot of grass in college, hadn't run across much hash, but he remembered the experience well. Susan King. Windy night. Rolling around in fallen leaves. The leaves running up and jumping over him. Her freckles up close. White stars on a blue shirt. The smoke was like perfume, like something from what he imagined an opium den to be, maybe a harem. The next day she told him that was not what she had meant at all. Not at all.

Culp wasn't sure what to do.

Obviously, these guys had used this room before, and now just rolled on in as usual—not noticing him up in the top bunk—and now, in their hash-heightened state, they were deeply focused on the view from the window, a surreal landscape, oddly pink and shimmering in the crazy street lights, lonely strangers in a strange land light years from home, sharing an hallucinogenic moment and oblivious to the room behind them. Culp cleared his throat.

Both men started so violently that the smaller man nearly fell out of the window, and probably would have if the big man hadn't grabbed him and flung him headlong into the middle of the room. The big man turned and was ready to fight whatever was coming. But he still couldn't see Culp in the dark on the top bunk. He looked around the room and at his friend on the floor. Now he was confused. Stoned and confused.

Culp sat up and swung his legs over the side of the bed. Both of the men grunted like they'd been hit. Culp reached for the light switch, but changed his mind. "I'm Culp. Got to Germany today, sleeping in the transient room. Sorry to interrupt you guys. Really."

There was silence. Then a giggle, the guy on the floor. Then both took turns saying *shit* in breathless voices. They said it at least twenty times each, sometimes overlapping, sometimes taking turns, or in little bursts of three or four *shits* in row. The big man staggered over and fell on the floor with his friend, rolling around like they were wrestling, and they laughed until they were out of breath. Finally they sat up on the floor, gathering themselves, giggling and looking up at Culp.

"It's like a gift, man," the little one said. The big man laughed. "No, no, don't you see? It's like, we were fucking busted, in the fucking jail, doing time, dishonorable discharge, fucked for fucking good, and then—we're NOT!" He fell back laughing and holding his stomach, and then sat up very straight and asked, "Do you get it, T? It's a gift. From God, man, from God."

"Yeah, yeah, I get it. Whatcha say your name was, my man?" Culp told him.

"Well, Cup, what's your MOS? You MP?"

"No, I'm 91Golf, Behav—counselor. I'm a counselor, you know, like Mental Hygiene."

"Hey, baby, we ain't going to jail, but I know somebody who is," the little one squealed like a kid who knows a secret.

"That right? You going to work over at the stockade?"

"I don't know. I'm assigned to the 42nd MPs."

"Yeah, shit, that's us."

Culp thought about the hash. "You guys MPs?"

The little man snorted. "I'm a clerk. I work in the orderly room. But Thompson here's full-blooded military po-lice. Shit, he's a ass-kicking mother."

"Lotta hash over here, is it?" Culp said.

"More than you'd believe," Thompson answered. He stood up and faced Culp. He was six six and two hundred forty pounds at least. *Linebacker size*, Culp thought. *If he wants to kill me to keep me quiet about his hash, it'll be a snap. Like the snap of my neck.*

But Thompson put out his hand and introduced himself. "And this is my homeboy Johnny Johnson—"

"Call me J.J."

"—and, well, we're damn glad to make your acquaintance-ship. Instead of, like, somebody else, right, J.J.?" At which they both laughed.

J.J. stood up and felt of his chest and face like he might be injured and said, "You know, I think I kinda lost my buzz somewhere. Mm, what say we step over to window here and FTTB."

"FTT what?"

"'Fine tune that buzz'." Thompson reached under Culp's arms and lifted him down from the bunk like a child. He pinched Culp's belly playfully. "Time to push away from the table, Cup my man," and laughed.

The harsh smoke choked Culp at first. But soon he had a nice floating buzz from which all fear, all anxiety, all paranoia, all guilt was washed clean. The three men stared out the window a long time. *It must be very late*, Culp thought. Just then J.J. had a notion.

"P Street."

Thompson looked at him doubtfully.

"Yes, " J.J. whispered. "Yes yes yes yes yes yes yes yes yes yes yes P Street."

Thompson turned to Culp. "You wanna get laid?"

Culp looked back and forth doubtfully at the men. *Laid by who*, he thought? *Not one of these guys, I do fucking hope.*

"That's cool," Thompson said. "I'm treating Cup to piece. How bout that, Cup, let me buy you a lady?"

They took out their money and counted it while Culp changed into civilian clothes. There was some fairly heated discussion, something about twenty dollars owed one way or another, but soon they were striding across the company yard toward the back gate of the kaserne. Culp noticed that his companions walked a lot alike, long strides, quick steps. They were very nearly running, but not quite, their hands pushed way down into their fatigue jacket pockets, their eyes on the ground in front of them.

Back gates are never open after dark, but the MP on duty there knew Thompson and opened it for them. They turned onto a long, dark street and took off like greyhounds. Culp had trouble keeping up. "How far to P Street?"

"About fifteen miles, I'd say. Wouldn't you say, T?"

Thompson smiled over his shoulder at Culp. "About that."

In a couple of minutes they rounded a corner in front of a streetcar station where three taxis sat idling. They climbed into the first one. The driver looked over the seat at them and Thompson said, "P Street." Without a word the driver pulled away from the station and sped down the narrow street.

The taxi made a long hard right up onto the autobahn and Culp was pressed irresistibly and uncomfortably against

Thompson. When he could straighten up, he mumbled an apology.

Thompson shrugged. "Hey, man, these German taxis are something. These guys fly!" The man drove like a house afire. Culp was scared but enjoyed it, like a carnival ride. The autobahn, as it ran through the city, was as bright as daylight.

They stopped at some indistinguishable corner and got out. While his new friends leaned into the taxi to pay the driver, Culp wondered what time it was. Exhausted from a full thirty-six hours without sleep, Culp was shivering. Part of that was probably fear because he'd never—what? visited? bought? used? a prostitute before. Of course, this was not something he was going to tell Thompson and J.J., oh no. He didn't know if they were going to a "house" or what. Would they pick up someone off the street and take her somewhere? Where? Was Thompson serious about paying for him? He didn't have that much money and payday was still a ways off.

They pulled him along the street in their strange semi-trotting walk, and at the next corner Culp saw that the street entrance was blocked by two large wooden barricades set up in such a way that you had to step around one and then step around the other to get onto the street. On the outside barricade the words *Kinder Verboten* were painted. They stepped out onto a brightly-lit street a block long with another barricade at the other end. In every first floor window lounged women in slips and negligees and pajamas, every kind of woman, blondes, redheads, skinny, heavy, tall. They all beckoned to him and his new friends. J.J. and Thompson just laughed and followed along behind Culp who looked from side to side all the way down the block and back. Some of the women stood out on the street, leaning against the buildings, staring across the street, sometimes at nothing, sometimes at a potential customer who stared back across the street.

"Well?" Thompson lit a cigarette and propped himself against a wall. "Have you decided?" Culp shrugged helplessly.

"Now listen, Cup. This is not, I repeat, *not* the most important decision of your life. This place is open twenty-four hours a day, seven days a week. You *will* be back. Many times. So who is it going to be?"

She was the first woman he'd seen when they stepped onto the street. She stood in a tall window as if she were modeling the black underwear and short black T-shirt she wore. Culp nodded over at her, and he and Thompson walked over to the window.

She opened the window and leaned down. "Sirty mark," she said. Culp looked at Thompson and Thompson looked at her, raising his eyebrows. She shrugged. Thompson turned and counted out three ten-mark bills into Culp's hand. She shut the window and disappeared. A minute later she appeared at a door and beckoned Culp inside. Thompson caught him by the arm and said, "Don't give her no more now, okay? Give her this thirty marks and no more." Culp nodded and stepped inside. She pulled the door shut, locked it, and led him upstairs.

Culp followed the woman through a warren of low-ceilinged halls. Some of the doors were open. The rooms looked like Hollywood clichés of brothels. Soft pinkish lights, fluffy canopied beds, red wallpaper. Hers was pink and lace. There was a wide bed with big soft pillows and a beautiful multi-colored quilt draped over it. She sat instead on a low daybed next to the wall and took off her shoes and underpants. She hadn't had shoes on in the window so Culp assumed she put them on the come to the door. She looked over at Culp and said, "*Schnell*. You. Clothes, huh? Come on."

He sat on a chair and began removing his clothes. Suddenly aware of how fat he'd gotten in AIT, he felt shy and self-conscious. Though she wasn't his first girl, she was his first prostitute, and he was now so nervous he feared he wouldn't be able to get an erection. From pure fright he began to talk, not knowing if she could understand him. "I just got to Germany today. I'm not even sure what city I'm in. What city am I in?"

"Sirty mark," she said and turned her deep blue eyes on him. Whatever cynical, woman-of-the-streets clichéd look he expected to see in her face was not there. She just looked tired, and maybe a little sad. He picked up his pants, pulled Thompson's money out, and gave it to her. She shrugged and put the money into a drawer from which she brought out a prophylactic. "*Kommen Sie,*" she said, and motioned for him to come to the narrow daybed. She took his limp penis into her hand and began to rub it. He put his hands on her waist and moved them up under the little shirt. "You want pretty good fuck, yes?" Culp nodded and she pulled the shirt up to reveal one breast. Culp was stiffening and he wanted her to take off the shirt. "Swanzig mark," she said and pulled the shirt back down, without releasing her grip on him. He didn't know what she meant, but he had twenty dollars in his pants so he gave them to her and she took off the shirt and put the rubber on him and lay back on the daybed. She pointed to something that looked like a light switch on the wall and said, "Doan toush, okay?" and he said okay and she guided him inside her.

Before he knew it it was over with. She slipped out from under him and hurriedly dressed. She led him down the stairs and let him out onto the street without a word. It was late, like a hundred o'clock or something. He looked around and saw Thompson across the street watching a girl doing a slow turn in a tall window, occasionally pulling up her baby doll nightie to show Thompson her red hugging panties. Up and down the street men in long overcoats leaned against walls and stared across at women who stared back or cut their eyes away, bent to straighten stockings, blew kisses. He crossed the street and stood beside Thompson.

"Where's J.J.?"

"Getting' some other end of the block. C'mon." Thompson shook his head at the girl and she shrugged and sat in a cane chair in the tall window. They walked slowly down the middle of the street, and Culp asked if Thompson was going to go with a woman.

"Nope. Married now. Used to though. Nothing wrong with it. It's legal and it's healthy. But I just don't now. Married."

Culp nodded. "She made me wear a rubber."

"Oh yeah, you can count on it. No amount of money gonna get rid of that rubber. At least no amount *we* got. You buy a blow job, you still gonna wear a rubber, no shit. Waste of money, blow job is. Don't bother."

Thompson led him to the latrine, the *pissoir*, he called it, a brick wall about midway down the block. They went behind it and pissed on the wall. Thompson looked at Culp. "Have a good time?"

"Yeah, thanks. I never bought a whore before. I saw a few at Ft. Sam, but it wasn't like this. They were standing on the street outside the back gate. I couldn't, you know, just walk up and well, you know—" Culp zipped up his pants and stepped around the wall.

"Anyway—this girl tonight was beautiful and all, but she just laid there. She was too passive or something. I don't know. It was weird. You know?"

"Hell yeah I know." He laughed. "You'll get used to it. You'll have to if you want any pussy at all. Cause the regular

German girls ain't gonna give it to you. Not without a lot of work. The Army girls all ugly or married or both." He stopped and took a deep breath. "The civilian Americans are all married dependents or jailbait, and all of them are stuck up. No, man, these girls here are all there is for us. Just remember where this place is and you'll be okay."

At the far end of the street J.J. stepped out of a recessed door tucking in his shirt and buttoning up his fatigue jacket. He saw them and clapped his hands and did a little Temptations turn. He cupped his hands and yelled at them. "Let's go get a beer!"

CHAPTER FOUR

13 July 1977, 1530 hours
Donner Strasse
Mannheim, Germany

When Carl started spending a couple of nights a week at the barracks, Lil didn't complain. In fact, she did everything she could to encourage him to. He missed his friends, the guards he worked with in the jail. After a couple of months, they had stopped coming to see him at the little apartment on Donner strasse. But they had not stopped coming to see her. The afternoon following their first little "get together" with some of the soldiers from his platoon, Sgt. Hampton, Carl's squad leader, dropped by, knocking on the door, saying *is Carl here*, knowing full well Carl's platoon, *his* platoon too, was on swing shift, and she knowing what he thought of her, what all Carl's friends thought of her, and even what Carl thought of her—dumb little hillbilly girl, country through and through, stupid, ignorant, a slut. She didn't know what Carl might be telling them about her. She got the feeling soldiers thought all women were sluts. But then again maybe they only thought she was.

Lil let Hampton in, let him drink Carl's beer, even let him kiss her, rub her breasts such as they were, and put his hands in her pants. But then she made him leave. The next day a different soldier showed up, some private. And the next another and the next another. She didn't let any of them in after Hampton. When Private Jennifer Styles showed up about a week later, Lil was glad, thinking maybe she would finally make a friend. But Jennifer told her all the guards were talking about her behind Carl's back and that several of them claimed to have fucked her. *Fucked her*, that's how Jennifer Styles put it. It was strange to hear such talk, man talk, coming from a woman. Then Jennifer Styles had pushed her down on the couch and kissed her, sticking her tongue deep into her mouth. Lil tried to push her off, but the woman, though skinny like her, was very strong, and the kiss wasn't that bad, so she let her kiss her some more and, after a while, even kissed her back some. It was nice, actually. Jennifer's lips were soft, and she kissed Lil in a hungry sort of way. They didn't "do" anything. Jennifer didn't even ask to go into the bedroom or anything. Lil told Jennifer she hadn't done anything with any of the guards that kept coming by while Carl was gone and Jennifer said she believed her, though Lil figured she didn't. When Jennifer was gone, Lil wondered if she'd go back to the barracks and brag that she'd fucked Carl's little whore too.

Actually she'd lied to Jennifer Styles. She had let one of the men who came by make love to her. Not fuck her. He had made love to her, in such a tender and kind way, that it had to be called making love. Hearing the word *fuck* come out of Jennifer's mouth, she understood finally what it was Carl had been doing to her since they'd been married. She had thought he was making love to her. *God, how wrong she'd been.* She was only fifteen when Carl had taken her from her father's house. *You're going with this here man*, her father had said, but she reckoned he owed Carl something, money or favors. Something. She had never been with a man in a sexual way, had never even kissed a boy until Carl. All she knew about sex was what she learned from him. So she had nearly made a fool of herself with Sgt. Cuthburt when they went together into the bedroom on his second visit while Carl was at work. She thought everybody dug through the dirty clothes before they made love.

The apartment was always quiet. Only very rarely did she hear anyone in the other apartments. Once she'd heard some kind of family dinner through the kitchen wall. But mostly she couldn't hear anyone. She knew people lived above, below, and beside them. But she rarely saw them in the stairwell, and when she did, they never spoke to her or even looked at her. Not that it mattered really, she couldn't speak any German. And they couldn't, or wouldn't, speak English. How can you make friends with someone you can't talk to?

After Carl finished basic training, he came home for a week. He had sold their house before he left, and so she had gone back to her father's house, taking up with cooking and cleaning for him as if she'd never been gone. The week Carl was home her father had given them his bedroom, and he had slept on the couch. She spent most of that week, night and day, tied up like a hog in her daddy's bed, in the stink of dirty laundry, Carl grunting on top of her. He said that the ten weeks without her had been hard, that he needed to get caught up loving. He told her he would have to go on for some more training somewhere, but after that she could come and live with him wherever the Army stationed him. And then he was gone again. Fourteen weeks, somewhere in Georgia. He never wrote.

Sleeping on the couch in those weeks, her father's snores rattling through the house, listening for her little brothers to cry out in the night as they sometimes did, she thought of her mother, five years dead now, burned up by fever, eat up by some cancer the doctor couldn't help, just a year after Jimmy was born, two years after Little Tommy. Lying there, waiting for Carl to come back for her, she missed her mother in way she hadn't before, in a way that grabbed her by her insides and twisted, and no matter which way she turned or how she hunched herself over and hugged that couch, she couldn't shake off that wanting. Tonight, Lord, it would be a blessing beyond all of it, for her Mama to sit down on the edge of the couch where she lay, touch Lil's hair, maybe sing in that peculiar off-key way she had. If she'd just kiss Lil goodnight, let her red hair fall around their faces, cover them like a tent, hiding their prayers and goodnight kisses like angel wings.

Carl hadn't come to get her after all. Instead he went straight to Germany after he finished his advanced training. Three months later, he sent for her like he said he would. She took a plane from Little Rock to New York and then on to Frankfurt, Germany. She never got off the plane in New York. She had heard bad things. It was a long flight to Germany, and she was tired when she got there. Carl did pick her up in Frank-furt, there had been some question about that. Good thing, too, because she was dead on her feet. He came to get her on the train. They had a heck of a time getting all her stuff to the train station and onto the train. She was so tired that everything she saw looked like a bed. She kept wanting to lie down right on the street. It was nighttime when they got to Mannheim and took a taxi to this place she now lived, the little apartment on Donner strasse. It all seemed like a dream. The streetlights cast a pink glow on everything, the streets were empty, not a light on in any house as far as she could see in both directions. All she wanted was to get into bed and sleep. But, of course, that wasn't what Carl wanted.

No, of course not. That first night in Germany—and she beat down like a threadbare rug—he had to get "caught up loving." He went at her for an hour and then rolled off her. She thought maybe he was done, but no. He tried again for about fifteen minutes, then he untied her and turned over and went to sleep. Not so much as a by-your-leave.

In a few minutes she got up and went to the bathroom. Her reflection in the mirror was something out of a horror show, but there was no hot water to wash her face. She went ahead and washed her face in cold water and dried herself with a stiff towel that smelled like Carl. Then she plopped down on the bathroom floor and cried. Hundreds and hundreds of thousands of miles from Arkansas. Lord have mercy, even her daddy's poor house had hot water.

CHAPTER FIVE

13 July 1977, 0030 hours
77th MP Detachment Barracks
Coleman Kaserne
Mannheim, Germany

Sergeant Jack Stuart pulled aside the curtain and looked out at the brightly-lit company yard. The street lights pitched sharply angled shadows of the towering pines around like some old German movie. It was two months since they'd found Watson dead. Two months of talking to the Criminal Investigation Division, the MPs, the battalion commander, the commandant of the jail, the company commander. Hell, any officer walking across the kaserne felt free to stop him and ask him about the situation. His story never changed. The medical officer confirmed death by strangulation and agreed that it was possible for the prisoner to have hanged himself in the manner his position in the cell indicated. Stuart had gotten a lot of stories straight over the past three years. He'd never hesitated to cover the fuck-ups of his platoon. He'd covered their fighting and drunkenness, their hash and their Mandrax. He'd even covered an AWOL. Of course, that had been for Jessie. But this Woods business was just too much. Woods had murdered the son of a bitch. Just cold-blooded murder. Two guards on Woods' shift had said as much. But

Stuart scared them both bad enough to keep their mouths shut. However scared they were of the CID, they were a hell of a lot more scared of Stuart. *And with good reason*, he thought.

But he'd been having second thoughts. Why had he gone to all that trouble for a bastard like Woods. When Kearns called, panicked, desperate, Stuart had charged up the hill to the jail, stepped in, took over, and saved a guard's ass. It was instinct. He didn't think it through. But he should have thought it through. He had just wanted to protect guards. That's what Stuart did. Protect guards. He just wanted to help Kearns and Jernigan and Tony Jackson. Instead, he'd ended up leaving a psychopath on the job. Worse, he'd kept him out of jail. And jail was where Woods belonged.

Actually, in his heart, Stuart believed that Woods belonged in a ditch somewhere with a bullet hole behind his ear. Some people simply did not rise to the level of human being. Of *human* being. They were beings, all right, people of some kind, but they weren't human. *Untermenchen*, the Germans would say. There are different kinds of them: sociopaths, psychopaths, morons. And killing them was not always wrong. In fact, sometimes, killing them was the exactly the right thing to do. Except that Stuart couldn't kill Woods. But if he could go back, he'd damn sure let Woods go to jail for killing Watson.

Instead, Stuart had gotten Woods transferred off Second Platoon. Now he was on Fourth. Fourth Platoon had not been Stuart's first choice. The man had to be moved, no question— but to Chambers' platoon? Stuart worried that he had inadvertently made things worse.

The guard shift would change at 0100 hours and a few minutes later the men from Chambers' Fourth would come spilling down the hill from the stockade. They would stay up all night, drinking, yelling, running up and down the halls, blasting their music at full volume, and harassing unmercifully the soldiers working other shifts who would be trying to sleep and those from the First Platoon, his platoon, who were now off for three days.

His room in the barracks was small, but it had been his choice. He had told the then-company commander, Captain Christopher, that he would take the room nobody wanted: his selflessness in that matter earned him a big favor from the captain, the first of many. That was—God, three years ago! How had he stayed so long? Taking the small room allowed him the luxury of solitude: during the worst overcrowding in the barracks, he never had a roommate. It wasn't even a possibility. Small room. Anyway, he didn't need a lot of space. A small lamp, its shade covered by a towel, cast a dim golden light. He had turned off the bright fluorescents. There was enough light to move around in, but not enough for anyone passing his door to think he was in there. He didn't want any company tonight. He needed to think.

Dominating the view from his window was the jail. The United States Army Area Confinement Facility at Mannheim. His since 1974. The place was hugely lit up, a sinister glow in the night, like a city on fire on a hill. Originally built by the Nazis, and miraculously surviving the leveling of wartime Mannheim, it was seized by the American Allies and put to its intended use, confinement of military personnel. It was surrounded entirely by double fencing topped with concertina, a particularly vicious version of barbed wire dotted with, instead of pointed barbs, something akin to razor blades. Guard towers stood on the four corners of the enclosure and were manned by angry, shotgun-wielding guards, one to a tower. Nobody wanted that duty. Stuart rotated the posts equitably throughout his platoon, at least up to the rank of E-3. He knew for a fact that Sgt. Chambers of the Fourth Platoon routinely used the towers to punish his guards. Boots not highly polished, uniform not starched to cardboard stiffness—tower duty. But then again, Chambers' Fourth Platoon did always look damn good, totally sharp, totally strack. No doubt there were other ways to get on Chambers' shit list. No doubt.

No doubt either that Stuart had to get off the guard platoon. Three years ago, arriving from Viet Nam after two tours as an MP in Saigon, he had liked this job. The men had accepted him easily. He found that the company and the jail ran by the Book. And if it was one thing he knew, it was the Book.

Before his induction, Stuart had been a lawyer. He had even run for the House of Representatives from his district in Virginia. But he got taught a lesson about the Ins and the Outs. He had come to understand, finally, that he was an Out and the Ins would never let him into the Club, much less to the House of Representatives. He got lied to, manipulated, and cheated. It had angered him then. He'd raised hell. Then the Ins got him drafted: a forty year-old lawyer with a heart murmur and arthritis in both knees drafted as an enlisted man. He'd tried to fight it and lost. They wanted him out of the state, and they got him out, all the way to Viet Nam. He supposed they must have wanted him dead. He shook his head now in wonder at his own naiveté.

He understood now. Too late, of course. *I have had to learn the simplest things last. Which made for difficulties.* Now he lived by one maxim. *Knowledge is power.* For all his education and his native intelligence back then, he knew virtually nothing. But now he knew all the angles. He was a born tactician. Just like his namesake, James Ewell Brown Stuart. The Confederate general J.E.B. Stuart. His own daddy had claimed to be a direct descendant of the great man. Naturally, as a youngster,

Jack read everything he could about the general. Lord, what a dandy! Oscar Wilde on a horse waving a sword. Sat the saddle like he was a knight, riding down from the Middle Ages, lance decorated with women's garters. But also a born tactician. The greatest, in fact, of the War Between the States. Once he led his troops all the way around the Union Army to hit them from behind. When the South lost him, they lost the war.

At one time, back in Viet Nam, he'd planned to go home, run for the House again, show them all. But not now. To succeed—well, to succeed you needed to know the angles, and the only angles he really knew were Army angles, so he stayed. And once he'd decided to stay, he could have gone to Officer Candidate School. He *was*, after all, college educated. And then some. But the Army regulations, especially those governing the Uniform Code of Military Justice, Military Police, and now the Confinement Facility, made clear to him that he could accomplish much more as a sergeant, an E-5 or E-6, than he ever could as a first or second lieutenant. Anyway, he liked being enlisted. That way he could have all the authority in the world delegated to him, and he often did, but he could never take on the responsibility. Ultimately, only officers could be responsible. Yes, he knew the angles, knew the regs backwards and forwards. The present company commander was almost tragically dependent upon Stuart for his knowledge of and ability to interpret the regulations. And thereby the captain's ability to run the company. That dependence gave Stuart much of the power he presently enjoyed.

From his window Stuart saw several figures emerge running from the darkness between the jail and the barracks. Fourth Platoon hotshots anxious to get into their civilian clothes and out on the town. A few minutes later a larger group of the guards appeared and moved slowly toward the barracks. Then a few stragglers, barracks rats who had no plans and nowhere to go. They'd spend the night watching TV in the dayroom, surreptitiously drinking beer, hounding the CQ and his assistant before staggering off to their rooms. Finally a lone figure emerged from the darkness. Stuart peered through the dusty glass at the silhouette moving without hurry toward, then past the barracks, and off into the night again. Probably Chambers, yet another *untermench*. Yes, Stuart *had* to get off the guard shift. The administrative platoon was soon going to need a new platoon sergeant. It was time to make his move.

CHAPTER SIX

14 July 1977, 0630 hours
42nd MP Group
Drexel Kaserne
Mannheim, Germany

The assistant CQ woke Culp at 0630. His face was flushed and his birthmark seemed darker than the night before. "Don't let the Top Sergeant scare you. Your duty assignment is not his decision. You're gonna go where you're gonna go."

The MPs in the latrine barely took notice of Culp and went about their usual morning routines. Fit, muscled, and unashamed of their bodies, they walked up and down the hall naked. After he showered and climbed back into his Class A uniform, Culp made the bunk as tightly as he could, borrowed a broom, mop, and bucket, and scrubbed down the floor, though the guys he got them from said he didn't need to bother cleaning transient quarters.

He made his way back to the Orderly Room. As he crossed the company yard, the MPs who'd been lounging around, smoking and talking, were called to attention and they snapped into perfectly dressed lines in three formations, the three platoons Culp supposed the company must be divided into. The platoon sergeants moved among the ranks inspecting uniforms and haircuts. There was a fair amount of ass-chewing going on, and Culp rubbed the back of his neck. He needed a haircut. His uniform looked like it had been slept in, as indeed it had been. Except for last night, he'd been in the same uniform for the past forty or so hours. The last thing he wanted was to be inspected by some Military Police platoon sergeant who wasn't satisfied by *this*, the meanest, cleanest, best-looking bunch of soldiers he'd ever seen. So he slipped up the steps of the Administration building and into the Orderly Room, praying he didn't run into the First Sergeant coming out.

The Orderly Room had a counter that ran from one end to the other, behind which sleepy clerks sat at desks over cups of steaming coffee, heads in hands. Culp looked around—no Top Sergeant in sight—and cleared his throat. No one looked up.

"Formation outside," Culp said. He paused. "Going on now."

A bleary-eyed PFC turned his head and said, "Admin formation was at 0630." With that he put his head down onto his desk with a thud and said no more.

"I guess I missed it," Culp mumbled. Then brightly, "I'm supposed to see the First Sergeant." No one responded. He walked farther down the counter. "Excuse me."

"What? What is it?" An irritated female clerk snapped her head up and eyed Culp like he was a roach that had crawled up onto her strudel.

"I'm supposed to see the—"

"First Sergeant ain't in yet, take a seat."

"Will he—?"

"Sit down, shut up, and hush! Can't you see I got a headache?"

Yes, Culp thought as he surveyed the chairs on his side of the counter, *the clearly visible headache, I don't know how I missed it.* He selected the most comfortable looking chair, and though it groaned mightily when he sat down, it didn't collapse, so he was able to perform in relative comfort the only job for which the Army had thoroughly and perfectly prepared him: waiting. The First Sergeant didn't come at 0730 nor at 0800. 0900 and 1000 hours came and went in slow succession and still no Top. In that time the Orderly Room picked up its pace some, more coffee was made and drunk, though none was offered, typists typed, papers got shuffled and filed and shuffled some more. Still no First Sergeant. But this did not bother Culp. He felt he could, if need be, spend the next two years of his enlistment waiting, in the Orderly Room of the 42 MP Group (Customs), live in the transient room, become a fixture, run errands, make friends, be accepted. Any postponement was preferable to facing whatever unknown horrors came next.

At 1130 hours, one of the more personable jerks told him the First Sergeant probably wouldn't be in until after lunch and why didn't he go have something to eat and come back around 1300. Okay. He went back to transient room and then remembered that he forgot to ask where the mess hall was. It didn't matter since he had no appetite. He damn sure didn't want to wander around the place, kaserne or whatever, trying to find it just so he could try to get fed on his traveling orders, probably get hassled about not being from one of the local companies, almost for sure have to sit alone. Too much for the old stomach. *I've got the least appetite of any fat guy I know*, he thought and almost laughed. No. Better to wait here in the privacy of the transient room, read a little, and hope maybe the First Sergeant wouldn't come in this afternoon either.

Jessie sat on the small balcony of his house. It was a beautiful two-story house on a typically small lot surrounded like every other lot on the block by a waist-high brick fence. The balcony faced south and looked across the steep orange-tiled roofs and the lush verdant squares that were the backyards of the village of Lampertheim. In the distance he could see the sun glinting gold off the lazy Neckar. The sky was completely clear, a hard cobalt blue. It was breezy and so a little cool here on the south side of the house, but he was comfortable. His luxurious maroon silk robe and the rich steaming coffee brought up the outside steps by his neighbor worked together to—let's say, *comfort* him. Yes, he was comfortable, comforted by luxury.

As Omah ascended the steps again, this time with some sweet, sticky rolls she had made herself, Jessie pushed the balcony door open a bit to look inside. The sleeping forms of several of last night's partygoers were strewn about the room as if flung there by some angry giant. Across couches, on the floor, in chairs, on tables. In the corner under the stereo cabinet a young soldier lay naked in the arms of an equally naked German woman, vividly hennaed and at least old enough to be his mother, both having apparently passed out in the act. The soldier's face—his name Jessie could not remember—was pure and sweet and lay on the woman's breast so serenely that Jessie wished he had a talent for painting. An oedipal pieta.

Omah put the sticky rolls down and smiled at him with an obvious affection that, at least it seemed to Jessie, went beyond the ridiculously large amount of money he paid her every month for breakfast and cleaning. He beckoned to her and bussed her on the cheek. She blushed and chattered some rapid fire German. He offered her a crisp, blue fifty-mark note, which she accepted without looking at—*vielen dank*—and slipped it into the deep pocket of her colorful, quilted apron. He watched her make her way down the stairs and through the gate into her own yard, a yard with the requisite eight by eight foot square of perfectly manicured grass surrounded close to the fence by an odd mixture of flowers, bushes, and vegetables. A beautiful rose shone in sunny competition with a beefsteak tomato as big as a softball. His own yard was as full as any other. The one unforgivable sin in German yards was to leave any ground untilled. *Really*, he thought, *that's true about all of Germany.* Every space has a use, every piece of ground a purpose. Soccer field closely bordered by someone's garden, military kaserne next to a paper mill, gasthaus next to private home. Even the woods that bordered his neighborhood were planned. They had a purpose. The endlessly efficient Germans had cut paths in straight lines through the woods to facilitate citizens' constitutionals. Oh, the Germans were big ones for walking. One in search of the road less travelled could, if so inclined, strike off through the woods in any direction, but would eventually cross one of the planned paths. Even a simple walk through the woods was according to someone else's plan. A path could never just evolve through use. Given woods, people would find the best way through, and with consistent use, that way would eventually become a path. But German paths were planned, on a grid probably, and, offered a path, people usually took it rather than finding their own way. No piece of ground was left to discover its own purpose. Jessie rarely saw land in transition from one purpose to another. Purposes had been established a long time ago.

When he finished the coffee, he went inside and locked the door to the balcony and pulled the curtain. No point in these people getting any ideas about room service. When he went to work today (and he *was* going to have to go to work today because Lewandowski, the company clerk, had called him this morning to say a new replacement had arrived in the night and was bound for the 77th MP Detachment over at the Coleman Kaserne, and that meant the First Sergeant would want Jessie to drive him), yes, after he left for work, Omah would come over within five minutes and run off the whole sick crew. He'd never see most of them again. Perfect.

He picked his way across the living room to the bathroom. He'd had the bathroom refurbished, the only room in the house he'd really done anything to since he bought it. He had liked the tub, longer and deeper than the usual American version, so he kept it, though he'd had a shower installed. But the toilet! The German one that had been in the place before had a little shelf down in it upon which one shat. Then flushing was a matter of the water running across the shelf and sweeping the business down the drain. He had spent some time thinking about the shelf and about the kind of people who would want their feces so well displayed for examination before disposal. He'd talked to Stuart about it. Stuart had a theory, but then Stuart had a theory about everything. Finally he had the toilet replaced with a regular one. It was just too weird.

He took a long shower and put on a pair of permanent press fatigues. He got his field jacket and cap headed for the bus stop at the corner. He waved at Omah coming out of her house with her long broom. Then the richest man in the United States Army climbed onto a crowded, over-warm bus and rode toward Mannheim.

Culp sat on a bench outside the orderly room, waiting for his ride, and read his worn out copy of *The Portable Nietzsche*. The purple cover and most of the pages had come apart. He kept it all together with a rubber band. It had seen hard use, especially through Basic and AIT, the cover crumpled so many times it looked like a detail map of the tributaries of some purple river seen from impossibly high.

The encounter with the First Sergeant of the 42nd MP Group (Customs) had been a breeze. He had come in after lunch and met with Culp immediately. He had actually apologized and explained about his morning at Finance trying to get his pay straightened out. Then he gave Culp ten copies of a new set of orders assigning him to the 77th MP Detachment. The 77th was attached to the United States Army Area Confinement Facility at Mannheim, which was really just a long name for the biggest military stockade in Germany. The 77th had a standing request for counselors. He wished Culp good luck and told him to wait outside for a jeep to take him to Coleman kaserne over on the south side of Mannheim. Culp asked him where he was now, and the First Sergeant said he was presently on Drexel kaserne which was on the north side of Mannheim. Culp had wanted to ask more, but the First Sergeant was obviously through with him, so Culp took his orders and went back to the transient room. He got his duffle bag and suitcase and went outside to wait for his ride.

Though the air was pretty cool for July, there was no wind where he was and the sun was beating down on him pretty good in his Class A's. He was very tired of this uniform, and just plain tired too. He wondered if he would ever see Thompson or J.J. again. Anything was possible. Culp hadn't made any friends in the Army, but then his assignments so far had been ten weeks apiece. How do you make friends that fast? And then keep them after they go to Kansas and you go to Germany? Just no way. At least he'd be at the 77th for a while.

The 77th MP Detachment. The United States Army something something Confinement thing. What now? What new terrors was the Army about to throw at him? AIT hadn't been too bad, more like a strict school than the Army, but Basic had been a nightmare. In Basic he'd told himself over and over that if it just didn't kill him, it would make him stronger. Now he thumbed through the grimy pages of his *Nietzsche*. Some phrase of comfort. No. Some phrase of indomitable strength. His eyes fell on a passage in *Zarathustra*: "Oh, lonely one, you are going the lonely way to yourself." A jeep horn sounded, so close that he nearly fell off the bench. He looked up into the most beautiful face he'd ever seen, smiling at him from the idling jeep.

"Need a ride, soldier boy?" Jessie said.

"I used to work at the jail myself. A guard, God help me." Jessie drove with one hand once he got the jeep into fourth gear. They had driven on the autobahn for a few miles, and then got off and seemed to turn completely around, and were now driving on a lonely stretch of road that was slowly rising. They bounced through a tiny village, on streets barely wide enough for the jeep to pass. Beyond the village the road rose steadily into a pine forest until they reached the top of what Culp would have called a mountain, but what Jessie called a great hill. They pulled over to the side of the road and Jessie got out and stood on the hood, taking a good look at the view.

"Where are we?" Culp climbed out of the jeep and stood looking up at the driver. "Are you taking me to the 77th?"

"Don't worry. I'm just taking the scenic route." Culp's face must have looked less than relieved, so Jessie said, "It's all right. I know someone at the 77th. You're Administration, right? I know the Admin platoon sergeant, we're P's, no problem. Come on up." He reached down a hand to Culp and pulled him up.

"I'm a counselor, actually."

"Not really. Are you? Well, then you're definitely on Admin platoon. In fact, you'll be working with Jack in the Counseling office. He's the NCO in charge."

"Who's Jack?"

"Jack Stuart. He's the Admin platoon sergeant and he's the head of the Counseling office, such as it is."

"Such as it is?"

"When I was there, the counselors were mostly knuckle-head guards working temporary duty as counselors. So what do you expect? No training. Just more of the same old guard bullshit in the Counseling office as everywhere else in the jail."

High, thin cirrus covered the sky, dimming the sun just enough to darken the woods around them and steal the heat. The trunks of the trees were black and Culp was suddenly chilly and afraid. He sat down on the hood and shivered.

"I'm kinda scared of this whole—I don't know—jail thing." He looked at his hands. Jessie sat down next to him. "This is a great job you've got. Just riding around all day, is that what you said? Yeah, that's great. How'd you get out of working at the jail? I take it you didn't like it very much."

"Hated it. The worst. But don't worry. See, I was on a guard platoon. That, my friend, is misery unmitigated. But you'll be on Admin. And Stuart will take care of you. He watches over his flock. He guided me through the valley of the shadow many times when I was on First Platoon with him. He was First Platoon leader before he went to Counseling. After I left, well, there was no reason for him to stay on a guard platoon." He laughed at his joke, but Culp thought there could be truth in it. This Jessie was not like anyone else he'd met in the Army. He was handsome and intelligent and seemed totally unafraid. Culp wanted desperately to be his friend, to see if there was any room under whatever umbrella of good fortune was over him.

Jessie patted him on the shoulder and suggested they get some lunch, though it had to be nearly five o'clock. Culp wondered whether there was any time by which he should arrive at the 77th. The Fear welled up in his stomach, but he pushed it down and got into the jeep, and they drove down into the little village they had passed through earlier.

Jessie led him into a travel poster gasthaus, brightly lit, where Germans drank murky beer from elaborate steins. The proprietor and his wife greeted Jessie warmly and ushered him and Culp through the dining room and then through the kitchen and down some stairs toward, it seemed to Culp, the basement. Instead, they entered a cavern-like room dimly lit by candles in red holders, one on each table. At the end of the room was a tiny stage next to an upright piano. The manager seated them at a table against the wall. They were the only customers in the room.

"Ham sandwiches okay?" Jessie said to Culp, as the proprietor brought sandwiches and two steins of beer to the table. The man said, *"Mit senf, "* and left. Culp's eyes were beginning to adjust to the gloom. The walls were decorated with posters of bullfighters and twirling dancers. A Rome poster. A *Maltese Falcon* poster with Humphrey Bogart glaring down. "Always order your ham sandwiches *mit senf*. It means 'with mustard'. Otherwise they'll make them their way, with butter. Whoa. Bad sandwich."

"Mit senf, " Culp repeated.

"Reading Nietzsche, I see. What?"

"Um, well, *Zarathustra*, right now," Culp mumbled through his sandwich, "but I've read this whole book, some parts of it many times."

"I'm impressed. You like *Zarathustra* I take it. Man is a bridge, and all that."

"I guess. It's more like poetry. Some of the other pieces are hard to follow."

"Like?"

"Well, like *Twilight of the Idols*. There are places where I just don't get it."

"What is it you like about old Friedrich?"

"I don't know."

"Well, do you agree with, for instance, his position on war?"

"I'm not sure I know it."

"Or his ideas about women?"

"It's not so easy to pin down what he meant—"

"OR—you like the idea of the individual, striving, alone, breathing the cold air of philosophy unfettered, the great spirit scorned by his own age." His voice louder and mockingly dramatic.

"Well—"

Jessie stood and addressed the empty room with a sweep of his arms. "The scientist of the human spirit, reaching deep into murky waters, pulling up the cold, unforgiving frogs and snakes of unspeakable truth, the Byronic hero, the solitary man, the James Dean anti-hero, choosing his fights carefully, the bridge, the maker of his own morals, the escapee from the prison house of language, the breaker of the manacles of the mind. Is that you, Culp?"

"You're making fun of me."

"Not at all. As Nietzsche himself might have said, Nietzscheans are like Christians: there are none. Or rather, there was only ever one of each. I like Nietzsche too, you know. It's just hard to live up to the ideal, hm, if that word could be applied here. But it goes beyond a rejection of Christian morality and metaphysics. That is just the first step, and since it's such a profound one, most aspiring Nietzscheans never get past it. That fatal first step." Jessie sat down, and Culp slumped in his chair and drank the strong, bitter beer. He couldn't finish the little sandwich. His stomach was in knots. Jessie ate both sandwiches and drank another beer.

When they stepped outside, the sun was streaming over the mountain, the last of the light casting the landscape into bas relief, every item in the village, the houses, the trees, the cars, the people gilded by the slanting light. They climbed into the jeep and descended from the village into the valley of the Neckar onto the plain where the city of Mannheim stood.

It was the dark edge of twilight when they reached the barracks of the 77th MP Detachment on Coleman kaserne. Where Drexel kaserne had looked very German, two- and three-story buildings with steep roofs, Coleman was very Army. Low sprawling buildings, jeeps and deuce-and-a-halfs parked in dressed columns, dust everywhere. "Army," Culp said as they drove slowly through the narrow streets.

"Yes. Very much so. Coleman kaserne is mostly infantry. Some air support, engineers, and communication companies. And the jail. It's the Army, all right. That's why I had to get out. Over to Drexel, it's more like a college campus than a kaserne. Mostly Admin, support for the general's staff housed there."

Culp was puzzled. "The general's staff?"

"The highest ranking general in this part of Germany is stationed at Drexel kaserne. Consequently, several high profile full-birds gravitate around him. It generates a lot of staff, clerks, typists, personal assistants. And drivers." His smile was so bright Culp wasn't sure how to take it. They squeaked to a stop in front of a barracks building at the extreme end of the kaserne. Beyond the barracks on the other side of a tall chain link fence there was a nearly empty stretch of what looked like airport runways and, beyond them, woods. A street ran along this side the fence. It dropped through a low ravine before rising up the only hill on the kaserne and ended at the stockade. The low, brightly-lit building dominated the horizon, like a symbol in a novel. Several soldiers slouched on the steps of the barracks, and amid the laughter and talk Culp heard a couple of them call out to Jessie, *hey, how's it going, when you coming back?* Jessie ignored them and said, "End of the road." As Culp pulled his gear out of the back of the jeep, the lounging soldiers scrambled to their feet, buttoning their jackets, pulling on caps, some standing at attention, some slipping around the corner or back into the barracks. A man had crossed the street behind the jeep and now stepped up behind Culp and cleared his throat.

"At ease, men," he said in a soft voice, though that did not prevent the quick evacuation of the area. "Specialist Culp, I presume. You're overdue. Have trouble finding your way?" The voice emanated from the shadow beneath the bill of an olive-green fatigue hat. Darkness had fallen and the glow of the street lights made every object jumpy at the edges. The sergeant (Culp could see the black stripes of a staff sergeant now on the man's collar) leaned forward into his face. The man smelled strongly of beer. *My shit is weak*, Culp thought. He opened his mouth to speak, but then Jessie said, "Actually it's Specialist Livingstone, and I, Dr. Stanley, have found the overdue explorer. Or have I found an overdue library book? And what's all this drill sergeant stuff. The way I heard it, you'd gone soft since you got on Admin. Give this poor traveler a break, he's a failed Nietzschean."

The sergeant laughed, and when Jessie stepped out of the jeep, he locked him in a bear hug. "Can you stay a while?" the sergeant said.

"No, gotta go. Try to come over this weekend. I'm having a party."

"What a surprise. When do you not have a party?"

"Often, I don't. But do come. I may have a surprise for you. And bring Lord Byron here with you. You two can discuss the eternal return or the will to power or some such. Personally, I will take a more non-rational approach to wisdom, thank you. Oh, by the way," Jessie bowed formally and gestured toward the sergeant, "this is Sergeant Jack Stuart, your platoon sergeant."

Stuart pushed his cap back on his head and took a long, appraising look at Culp, as if thinking there must be more than meets the eye. Jessie drove off into the night, and Culp watched the red taillights disappear around a corner. Stuart threw an arm around Culp and led him up the steps into the barracks. "So, Byron—Byron is it?—you're a friend of Jessie's?"

CHAPTER SEVEN

11-17 August 1977
77th MP Detachment
Mannheim, later Heidelberg, Germany

Sometimes Jennifer Styles could not believe her luck. After twenty crummy months working in the stockade, she'd found herself on TDY, temporary duty with CID, and fallen into the job of her dreams. She was out of the jail now, free of the guards and the prisoners and that drunk, Sgt. Jones. She had an apartment in the old part of Heidelberg. Soon she might have someone living with her, someone in her head and in her bed.

The first fourteen months at the jail had nearly beaten her. There weren't many women guards in the 77th MPs. There were none on her watch. Her roommate, Carole Kelly, was on a different platoon, Fourth Platoon, under psycho Chambers. So she and Carole were on different shifts and almost never saw each other. When Jennifer had her three days off, Carole was moving to three days on the graveyard shift, eleven to seven. Besides, Carole was gone all the time, seeing some guy that she was keeping secret. She denied it, said she went out by herself, said she was alone when she was off traveling to Paris or Switzerland or down in the wine country in southern Germany. So Jennifer spent a lot of time alone in her room. She had stopped answering her door unless it was Sgt. Jones or the CQ because if one of the guards from her platoon knocked on her door, it was only to see if he could get his hands down her pants. That part of it was constant at first. She was lonely, but she couldn't make any friends. No one even made small talk with her. She could make no friends because it became quickly clear that every word spoken to her, however casual, every kindness, however small, every smile was just a necessary first step toward fucking her. Even these pretenses at friendliness stopped once they understood that she was not going to sleep with all of them or some of them or even one of them. Then they called her a lesbian and locked her out of the life of the platoon.

There was very little good duty for her, very few jobs within the stockade that were tolerable. Standing one of the forward gates was okay. Tower duty had been cold last winter, but at least she'd been alone. What was insufferable was working in the bays where the prisoners were quartered. Standing any post where she had to frisk prisoners was bad. Sgt. Jones seemed to enjoy assigning her to A Block. There she had to walk up and down between the bays of the rowdiest prisoners. They weren't overtly obnoxious to her. She was, after all, a guard who could have them thrown into D Block, into isolation on reduced diet, for any infraction. But she could hear them behind her back speculating on her sexual orientation, the size of her breasts, and on and on. And, of course, her brother guards told them all she was a dyke.

The worst were the latrines. The latrines in the open bays were also open. Prisoners were allowed no privacy of any kind, so the walls of the latrine were like walls of bars, that is, they *were* walls of bars. The showers were out in the open and the toilets were lined up where she could see every man at his most humiliatingly vulnerable. Perched awkwardly on the rims of the toilets because the seats had been removed (and probably were never there to begin with), the prisoners looked steadily at their feet. It was the one time they didn't meet her eyes. The male guards often stood outside the latrine, talking about the men sitting there and laughing at their discomfort, sometimes mocking the sounds and the faces they made. And the guards especially enjoyed seeing her walk past the latrine. They knew that she *had* to look in there. It was her *job*. To keep an eye on the prisoners. And she did it. She did not let her embarrassment or their shame stop her from doing her job. But it was terrible. These men she was supposed to be guarding, who would naturally hate her, as a guard, and who would also resent her as a woman, who would want her as a woman, and who would twist in the confusing, wrenching conflicting emotions of desire and bitterness and hatred, all while trying to empty their bowels right in front of her. But the guards knew what she was going through, what the prisoners were going through. Yes, they knew. Hell, anyone would. The difference was they enjoyed it. Normal people wouldn't.

So when the guy from CID showed up, pitching a new job, she listened.

She had been in Tower One in the middle of a long shift when she was unexpectedly relieved by a sullen PFC and told to report to the Assistant Commandant. The AC was a short, thin, near-sighted major with a crew cut and a Napoleon complex, Major Petty. She thought the name was funny, but nobody else seemed to get the joke. He stood when she entered the room and returned her salute. The other man did not rise. He stayed in his chair facing the AC, so she could only see his back.

"I'll need your office. I need to talk to Private Styles. In private." Major Petty hesitated a moment, long enough for the man to say, in a harder voice, "You can go now."

Petty opened his mouth to say something, but he shut it and his face flushed with anger. He picked up some papers from his desk and marched out the door without another look at either of them. The man still had not turned around.

"At ease, Styles."

She put her hands behind her back and tried to relax. What now? What trouble was she in?

But, as it turned out, she was not in any trouble. He invited her to sit down, in the Major's chair yet. They faced each other across the desk. She scanned the front of his uniform, something everyone in the Army did. He was a full colonel and his name tag said *Faust*. He was at least fifty, but his black hair showed very little gray and his face was handsome and completely unlined. He looked kind of like one of the characters in a soap opera she used to watch, a good bad guy.

"I'm here to strike a bargain with you," he said smiling.

"I get that, sir," she said, "No, I really do. Faust—the devil's bargain. What kind of trouble am I in, sir?"

"None. I'm from CID. You know what that is?"

"Criminal Investigation Division."

"Yes. I'm here to offer you a job. How do you like it here? At the stockade?"

"I have no complaints, sir."

He cocked an eyebrow and smiled wryly. "Yes. I'm sure you don't. Still, I'd like to offer you a position with my group. It may not be something you're interested in. I won't bullshit you, Styles. It's hard, and it's, well, somewhat dangerous. But—there are a lot of fringe benefits, and you may just have a knack for it. And I want you to know that if you turn me down, there will be no hard feelings, and it will not reflect on your record in any way. It will not appear in your 201 file nor affect your chances for promotion or assignment.

"On the other hand, if you do come with us, there is an immediate promotion to E-5, retroactive to the first day of this fiscal year. Sergeant Styles. Do you like the sound of that?"

She did. In the hour they talked, he explained the many benefits of the job. He was quiet and reserved. At no time did he leer or wink or touch her or indicate in any way that he was interested in her sexually. She'd never met a soldier, officer or enlisted, who didn't have sex on the brain first and foremost and at all times. She wondered if he was really in the Army at all.

Faust said he'd seen her in a bar, in the old part of Heidelberg, and that as he watched the soldiers in the bar hit on her one after another, he'd had an epiphany. Soldiers, he said, would do anything to get laid. He said it straight out. Just like a doctor or something. Not trying to move the conversation toward sex. Just a statement of fact: soldiers love pussy. Period. No long looks, no casual touch. And many of those soldiers, he said, were involved with drugs, were dealing drugs to other soldiers. Hash, cocaine, dogs. Dogs? Dogs were Mandrax, he explained, a downer like Quaaludes. These drugs were undermining the readiness of the ground troops in Europe. And it was difficult to stop because of some kind of "code of honor" among drug users. They refused to "narc" on each other. They'd rather go to jail than name their sources. Male undercover agents could infiltrate the groups, but in order to do so had to actually take the drugs, which more often than not compromised their testimony.

"But you, Corporal Styles, will revolutionize drug work in the CID.

"Soldiers will try to make any woman, regardless of what she looks like. But a woman as attractive as you, well, they'll kill each other to get next to you. You tell them that you are interested in drugs, that you want them to help you score drugs, and without hesitation they will get the drugs you want so that they can endear themselves to you."

Suddenly she wasn't so happy about things. She looked around at the tight little office, its green block walls, its barred window, the soft lamp the only light in the room.

"You want me to be a narc? Narcs get killed. Sir. I may not have the greatest job here, but unless there's a riot or some kind of hostage taking or something, I'm safe. Even with murderers and rapists all around me, I'm safe."

"There's a danger, Styles, but it's not what you think. Killed? No. You won't get killed. Narcs get killed because people find out who they are. Here we don't have that problem. You know how this jail works. You get a prisoner here in pretrial confinement for six weeks, he goes to trial, he comes back here, BAM, two weeks later he's back in the world at Leavenworth. He gets no chance to schmooze with his buddies about the beautiful narc who busted him. Oh, you may get a rep in Leavenworth. Hell, you may well become a legend there, the goddess of some kind of jailhouse myth. But unless you get incarcerated there, you're in no danger."

He paused and leaned back, his eyes steady on hers. "Here's the real danger as I see it. Your conscience. Some of the people you'll bust are scumbags, real dirtballs who should never have gotten into uniform in the first place. And you'll enjoy busting them. You'll enjoy seeing the look in their eyes when they go down. You'll enjoy knowing that they're going away for a long time and that you put them there.

"But some of them will be nice kids. Yes. Nice kids. Otherwise good boys who think that drugs are 'cool', that dealing drugs is romantic. It's 1977, Styles. The guys who come into the Army now, their heroes are the heroes of the counterculture. Their older brothers and sisters are contemporaries of the Beatles and the Rolling Stones and Abbie Hoffman and the Chicago Seven. They may be in the Army, but they're looking beyond the Army. And they are not willing to completely give up their counterculture lifestyles. Look in any barracks room on this kaserne, and what do you see? Black light posters, loud, expensive stereo equipment, incense burners, guitars. How many soldiers do you know who are hiding long hair under their hats? But they're not really scum. Not of the criminal mindset. Back in the world they might just be what they think they are. Romantic heroes, individualists struggling against an oppressive, controlling society, trying to find new ways of living and thinking by expanding consciousness through the use of drugs and meditation and Eastern religion and whatever. Hell, that's what America is all about. Individualism, freedom, new ideas and new ways."

Jennifer smiled. "You sound like you admire them."

"Admire them? Maybe. Maybe not. Or maybe I just understand them." Faust was quiet for a moment. "But you understand this, Styles. This is not America. This is the Army. And it wouldn't matter if we were in Fort Polk, Louisiana, instead of Mannheim, Germany. The Army is not America. The Army supports democracy, but is not a democracy. The Army supports a society of free individuals, but is not a society of free individuals. The Army is a repressive fascist regime. The Army doesn't want or encourage individualism or free thinking or consciousness raising of any kind. Because the Army has no need of individuals or raised consciousnesses. The Army exists so those things can exist in America. But the Army can't *be* America and protect America at the same time. And we have to get these people, these drug takers and drug dealers, out of the Army. When the Russians come rumbling down through the Fulda Pass, we can't have fighting units full of free-thinkers and stoned gurus facing them down. We have to have fighting men. And women." He smiled, kind of sheepish, she thought.

"My point is, some of the people you bust will be nice kids. Kids who trust you, kids who want you. Some of them may fall in love with you. Can you send a fresh-faced kid from Kansas who is head-over-heels in love with you to Leavenworth for ten years because you asked him to get you some dope?"

Jennifer Styles didn't know what to say.

"Don't worry. I'm not asking for an answer. It's a rhetorical question. It's philosophy. It's something to think about. You may not know the answer for a long time. Maybe not until long after this is all over. Who knows? But you'll have to weigh that against what's good for the Army and what's good for America. You might also want to weigh it against what's good for Jennifer Styles. But listen to what I'm going to say to you now."

And then he outlined the benefits.

And the bennies had been good. He'd been right. The bennies were real good. Three months she'd been in the job now and she was actually considering reenlisting when her hitch ran out this December. That would be less than five months now. For the last two years she'd sworn to herself, and anyone else who would listen, that when her enlistment was up, she was out. But now—well, things were different now.

At the end of her interview with Colonel Faust, she told him she would take the job. He urged her, gently, to take some time to think about it. She said she would and she did, but really she didn't need to think about it. She took her time—to give him the impression she was thinking about it, to show she was reasonable and could follow orders, even when they were just suggestions. But the bennies convinced her.

A week later she called him and told him she was sure she wanted the job, and he said fine, he'd come right over and get her. She was puzzled by that. When he arrived, she was at the jail on shift. The first sergeant called the stockade and told Sgt. Jones to send her down ASAP. Colonel Faust was in the company commander's office. The first sergeant was glaring at her, chewing his cigar, but holding his tongue. The office door opened, and Faust came out with Lieutenant Mosley, the company commander. Mosley handed a stack of orders to the first sergeant.

Colonel Faust spoke to Mosley first. "We're going to secure her gear now, Lieutenant. Private Styles, give the First Sergeant here your weapons card. We won't be coming back, and he'll need it to complete your outprocessing." Colonel Faust was in civilian clothes. Lt. Mosley saluted him anyway, which the colonel ignored, and Jennifer followed him out of orderly room toward the barracks.

"I'd like to take as much of your gear as we can with us now. I don't want you coming back here." She led him up the stairs to the third floor where the women were billeted. He pointed to a spot on the floor of the hallway. "Just pile all your web gear and whatever else belongs to the 77th right here in the floor. I've told the first sergeant to have it all picked up and to have you cleared from the company. I'll wait in the hall while you change into civvies."

It was the fastest transfer she'd ever seen. Or even heard of. She changed into some jeans and a sweatshirt and packed her duffle bag, her laundry bag, and her suitcase. She didn't have that much. The TV and stereo were Carole's. There were some posters on the wall that were hers, but she just left them. The colonel picked up the laundry bag, shouldered the duffle, and headed for the stairs. She looked around the room one last time. *Good riddance*, she thought.

Colonel Faust drove very fast. But Jennifer Styles felt safe. The Mercedes was clean and comfortable, and the sky was clear and the sun warmed her through the windshield and she could smell the leather of the seats and the colonel's aftershave. A few minutes later they were on the Autobahn, and he pushed the Mercedes up around ninety. Soon they were in Heidelberg. They made a few turns and finally stopped in front of a military kaserne.

"This is where I work. CID for the western part of Germany is headquartered here." He didn't turn in. "I just wanted to show it to you."

The colonel had promised her an apartment. Of her own. They drove to three different places around the city. He stood back at each place and let her look around. After they had seen all three, she asked if they could go back to the first, an apartment above a bakery in the old part of the city, on a cobblestone street, at the foot of the mountain on which the castle stood. It wasn't as big as the apartments in the newer parts of the city, but it had nice windows, high ceilings, and a great view of the street. She could tell he approved. He went down to the bakery, and she could hear his rapid-fire German as he closed the deal with the landlord.

"Well," he said as he came back up the stairs, "you're going to need some more furniture. I don't know what you'll want, though, probably you'll want to replace that bed." She looked at him carefully to see if now he would make some kind of move on her, but apparently it was just an innocent remark. "Here's five hundred marks. Spend it on a couch or lamps or something. Whatever you think. Remember, you're an American college student studying at the University of Heidelberg. Now let's separate all your military stuff."

They went through her clothes and pulled out all the OD green and khaki. Her boots, her T shirts, her wool socks. Then he took her military ID, her ration card, her stockade ID. They went through her papers, and he took all her orders since Basic and everything else military. He packed them all into her duffle and laundry bag.

"I'm sorry," he said. "I need to look at your letters."

She didn't have that many. Her parents were divorced, and she hadn't heard from her father in years. There were a few letters from her mother, most of them written to her while she was in Basic. Those he put into a large manila envelope.

"I have to take these. I promise they'll be safe. I'll take care of them myself."

Then they went through all of her clothes and what few books she had, looking for anything that hinted of the military. There were some stray papers, copies of old orders moving her from Basic to AIT and such. Faust took all those too.

Maybe he sensed that she felt disoriented and violated, her life being pulled away from her, because he suddenly suggested lunch. They went downstairs and out into the street. Stepping out into the old part of Heidelberg, they might have been in the Middle Ages. They left the narrow street and turned onto the main street of the old part of the town. Two blocks and the street began rising toward the castle, looming dark against the brilliant blue of the sky. They walked up only a bit and stopped at a gasthaus that the colonel said served great bratwurst. She'd never had bratwurst, and it turned out to be a pale sausage that was excellent when dipped in mustard.

Sitting across from him, Jennifer was suddenly self-conscious. She could see them through the eyes of the other customers. She and the colonel were probably tourists. A father and daughter. A man and his young mistress. But whatever, they did not look military. Her hair was down now, a style not allowed in uniform. His hair, though short, was what you would expect from a man his age. Young male soldiers were easily identified even in civvies by their military haircuts. But the vast majority of men Faust's age wore their hair this length whether they were in the Army or not. She looked around the room. The Germans were mostly leaning into their meals, ignoring them. Completely different from when she went places out on the German economy with soldiers. Then the glances, the nods, the curiosity, the blatant stares. Today, though, she felt—invisible.

"This is probably all a little disconcerting," he said, wiping his mouth, pushing away his plate.

"I keep expecting to wake up," she said, unsure what he wanted to hear. She wanted to be tough, strong, capable. But she wanted to please him too. "It's like a dream. It's like the Army mighta just turned into a great job."

"It's not a great job. But it's not a dream either," he said and smiled. "It's real enough. Are you finished? Let's take a walk."

They pushed on up the hill. The required physical training and daily two-mile runs made the climb easy enough for her; even so she was breathing hard when they reached the castle entrance. Faust took it like a mountain goat, talking easily, pointing out features of the mountain and the castle. They skirted the entrance and walked around to where the gardens overlooked the old part of the city and the Neckar River. The roofs shone red in the afternoon sun and the brown river glittered and reflected patches of blue here and there.

"I'm getting you a car." He didn't look at her, but stared absently at the view. "Not much of one, mind you, but it'll run.

I want you to be able to get around if you need to, though I think most of your work will be right here in Old Heidelberg. There are a couple of bars right near the university that soldiers frequent looking for frauleins, but you never know where you might need to go. Also, I want you to pick up all your mail at the 77th. Don't receive any mail at the Heidelberg address. Don't tell anyone back home or at the 77th where you're billeted now. I'm sure you have friends at the 77th. Don't invite them to the apartment. Don't meet them in bars, at the EM club, whatever. I'm sorry, but you're a civilian now. It's going to be tricky, walking the line between being military and appearing not to be. Your friends who know you as Army could get you into trouble with people who are not supposed to know that."

"A car?"

"Yes. But did you hear what I said? You don't have any friends in the Army anymore. You don't even know anyone in the Army anymore. You're going to have to forget all the friends you have made so far."

"The truth is, I hadn't made that many. Just Carole, my roommate. You can't make 'friends' with guys. They just want—"

"I'm sorry about Carole. This may be a pretty lonely job. I hadn't really thought that through. You may be able to make some friends among the students in Heidelberg."

"It's okay. I'm kind of loner."

"Anyway, I'm also putting you in for hazardous duty pay. Though this doesn't really qualify in the sense of jumping out of planes and such, I think I can get it approved. Of course, I'll get you a gasoline allowance since you won't have a ration card for gas. You'll receive BAQ and separate rations monies."

"How much is my rent against my BAQ?"

"You keep the BAQ. I'm paying the rent."

"You?"

"My office. I've already paid six months in advance. Told the landlords you were my daughter studying at the university. They may think you're my mistress. Doesn't matter, they'll forget that when they don't see me there regularly. And then we'll see. Things change. You may not want to continue this job. The funding could get cut. Your enlistment is up soon. But don't worry. If the project continues, I'll get the rent paid."

"Wow. I'm getting a promotion, which is more money. I'm getting BAQ and separate rations which is more money. I'm getting a car and an apartment, all paid for. No more uniforms, no formations, no CQ duty, no guard duty, no first sergeant, no PT or cleaning the barracks." She turned to face him. "C'mon, Colonel, what's the catch? Some general gonna show up every week or so looking to spend the night? Or who?"

His face was very serious. "That, I promise you, is never going to happen."

She believed him.

"So when do I sign my name in blood?"

He smiled. "I hope never."

CHAPTER EIGHT

20-21 August 1977
U.S. Army Area Confinement Facility
Coleman Kaserne
Mannheim, Germany

Stuart took Culp under his wing. At least that's how Culp felt about it. The jail was scary. The whole Army experience had been bad up to now, but the jail was worse. If Basic Training was the Army at its most intense, the jail was Basic all over again. To the tenth power. But where Basic was hard and long and exhausting and screaming drill sergeants and dirty and wet and tired and militarily precise, strack, super strack, the jail was hard and long and exhausting and screaming guards, but clean and waxed and polished and spit shined, and equally strack. Culp had hated Basic—he guessed everybody did—and now it was just more of the same. Formations, marching, PT, inspections, not only in the barracks but in the jail as well. The guards scared the shit out of him. They were big and mean and pumped up and pissed off all the time. They never relaxed. Walking down the company street, they looked ready to put down prisoner insurrections bare-handed. His only consolation was that the guards held no real power over him. He couldn't imagine how it must be for the prisoners. Well, he could imagine, but he didn't want to.

Little by little he settled into a routine. Stuart helped a lot. Let him ease into it. Gave him a couple of days off right at first so he could lounge around the barracks, get to know where things were, in the company, on the kaserne. The work, when he got to it, wasn't that hard, just a lot of it. He didn't do any real counseling. No intake interviews the way he had learned in his Advanced Individual Training after Basic. No referrals to psychiatric floors of military hospitals. None of Glasser's Reality Therapy. No Transactional Analysis. No warm fuzzies. No cold pricklies. No counseling. He just did paperwork. Lots and lots of paperwork.

Because every prisoner generated a stack of paperwork. Unit, charge, sentence, destination. But Culp was a quick typist. IBM Selectric humming, spinning out another form, get them in, get them out. The prisoners were only at this particular stockade a short while. It was really just a stopping off point. Very few prisoners stayed longer than two weeks. What happened was that soldiers got arrested somewhere out in the boonies, Garmisch or Furth or some other infantry hellhole, and then got court-martialed and sentenced. If the sentence required jail time, not just loss of rank and pay, then the soldier got shipped back to the world, either Fort Leavenworth or Fort Riley, Kansas. If the soldier was being dishonorably discharged as a part of his sentence, then he went to Ft. Leavenworth and served his time as a civilian. If not, if the Army was going to try to rehabilitate him, then he went to Ft. Riley. And that was bad. It was like a jail-operated Basic. Basic was bad enough. To be a prisoner *and* a trainee? Culp would rather be dead.

But Culp got acclimated. As miserable as he was, he could see how much worse off the prisoners were. And there were certainly worse places to be stationed in Germany. The jail was at least clean. Spic and span clean. In fact, it was absolutely the cleanest place Culp had ever been in his life. The main front administrative hall was constantly being cleaned. It was the cleanest, shiniest floor he'd ever seen. He could truthfully say, truthfully now, that he could eat off the floor. He did not doubt even for an instant that it was a hundred times cleaner than the mess kit he ate out of in Basic. And it was a damn sight cleaner than the plates at the Consolidated Mess. He never stepped out of the Counseling office that there wasn't a prisoner with a can of wax, or a buffer, or a mop and bucket working the front hall. Doubtless, some prisoner was mopping or waxing the floor on the graveyard shift while Culp slept. The whole thing was like the Golden Gate Bridge. As soon as you finished painting it, you go back to the other end and start over. Except with the bridge it made sense. The bridge takes so long to paint that when you finish, it really is time to start painting it again. But floors could be cleaned twice a day and they'd be immaculate. Clean them six times a day and they'd be the cleanest floors in the Army, in Germany, maybe in the world. But to clean them constantly? And it was the same all over the jail. Every office was constantly being cleaned. Even the Counseling office, though the activity got to Culp when he was trying to type up the endless paperwork generated by the endless parade of incoming prisoners, so he was always telling them to sit down, have a smoke, relax. The prisoners loved to clean the Counseling office. It was one of the few places they weren't constantly being harassed by the guards. They damn sure weren't going to get a cigarette break mopping the Admin hall.

But, of all the places in the jail, the mess hall was the cleanest. Culp had recently started taking his meals there. He had noticed that most of the facility's cadre ate in the jail's mess hall every day, breakfast, lunch, and dinner, and that seemed strange because the mess hall sergeant actually let a couple of the *prisoners* do all the cooking. After eating there the first time, though, Culp understood. The cadre got to eat first and got all they wanted, seconds, thirds, whatever they wanted in whatever proportions. And, oh, the food was good. It was the best Culp had ever had in the Army. He loved it.

In the barracks, Culp bunked with two clerk-typists, PFC Wilson and PFC Williams. But he never really saw them much. They didn't work in the jail. They worked in the Orderly Room. And they were rarely in the barracks. As soon as they got off work, they changed into civvies, nearly identical velour shirts and flared slacks hemmed long so the cuffs would fit with their four-inch platform shoes. They spent their nights in the discos in Mannheim and Heidelberg trying to get next to German women. And apparently with some success because they sometimes stayed out all night and dragged in in the morning just in time to stand formation. Which they sometimes stood in their civvies. Stuart never chewed them out, as long as they actually showed up. They never set foot in the jail, but had plenty to say about it. They had set Culp straight early on: guards hate prisoners first, counselors second, and anybody on admin platoon third. Stay outta their way. Culp had overheard—he figured he was supposed to—comments from guards about counselors coddling the cons. He'd even been confronted face to face by a drunken guard in the PX one night, a big ugly redneck named Woods. Screaming about maggots and faggots and Stuart and counselors, his baby fat face flushed and sweaty. Culp had beaten a hasty retreat.

Though not before noticing the redneck's wife.

She stood just inside the door of the little bowling alley adjacent to the PX, just eight lanes, never full, mostly empty, and she held a Coke can near her mouth, not drinking it exactly, more like she was hiding behind it and watching everything.

She was small and thin with long brown hair, and she looked very young. She could have been thirteen or fourteen years old, though Culp knew she had to be older than that. After he disentangled himself from the redneck, Culp hung around in the parking lot where he could still see her. He realized she was Woods' wife only after she brought him a beer and he pulled her down onto his lap. She sat there, hiding behind her Coke, while the big redneck completely ignored her.

It wasn't fair. Culp was a nice guy, decent looking, if a little heavy, and he hadn't had a girlfriend since—well, not since being in the Army, that's for sure. You couldn't meet girls in the Army. Not without a lot of trouble. What were your choices? Hanging out in the Enlisted Men's club? At the EM clubs there were a hundred guys to every one female soldier. Go out on the economy? Most of the German girls were too smart to get hooked up with soldiers or were at least smart enough to choose officers over enlisted. Wilson and Williams worked like dogs to get laid, spent every cent they made on clothes and transportation and cover charges and drinks for frauleins who mostly drank their drinks and then promptly forgot about them. Wilson had told Culp that the return on the investment was minimal. You worked twenty, twenty-five girls, and got one. If you were lucky.

Culp had spent some time in the EM and civilian clubs. Mostly just sitting and drinking, watching what few women there were. Any woman was the center of all attention. Only the boldest, the most persistent got close to them. At his most confident, Culp was still shy around women, relying on long looks and quiet conversation to convey his interest. None of that here. He could look around the EM club, the bowling alley, the PX and see the same story everywhere. Every guy there looking at some one woman, hoping she would look at him, maybe hold his gaze for a moment, the promise of something never to come, and then spending the next week masturbating and thinking about that look, that one short, sweet instant of female contact, however remote, however meaningless, however insignificant to her. With every stroke, the fantasy grew, the look became conversation, conversation became contact, contact intimacy. And then you were soaking your belly with cum, wiping your hand on the bed sheet, drifting off to sleep, spent but unsatisfied.

There was always P Street.

It wasn't fair.

And here was this big, drunk, ignorant, violent redneck, ugly as sin, and he had a pretty young wife he treated like shit. And here was Culp, no girl, no hope of a girl. Now Woods pushed her off his lap and leaned forward to tell his cronies something. About the jail, no doubt. The guards talked about little else, even off duty. She stepped back against the wall and looked over the guards' heads out the door toward the parking lot and their eyes met. She looked away quickly. Most women did. They didn't want to give you the wrong impression. Not that they cared about your feelings. They just didn't want to deal with you, tell you no, get lost, I'm married, whatever.

Or maybe she recognized him as the man her husband had yelled at, and she was embarrassed. Or maybe she didn't see him at all, just the glass of the door reflecting her own image back at her.

The guards all stood up and yelled, their bulldog grunting, Culp called it. The bulldog was the mascot of the jail. Not mascot, he thought, since they didn't actually have one, just a symbol. Then they rushed out of the PX and headed toward the front gate. Woods stayed behind a moment and talked to his wife, handed her something, money maybe, and then followed the others out, fortunately ignoring or not seeing Culp propped against a parked car. A couple of the guards came out afterward and turned back toward the barracks. One of them stopped and said hello to Culp. The other one just kept walking toward the barracks. *Doesn't mix with admin,* Culp thought.

"How's it going, Culp?" It was Sergeant Kearns who worked on First Platoon, Stuart's old platoon. Culp had found him to be a reasonable guy at work, didn't give him or the prisoners any unnecessary shit. Stuart had described him as decent, if dull.

"Just trying to stay alive," Culp said, watching the backs of the guards headed toward the front gate.

"Don't worry about old Carl. He's just drunked up and in a shitkicking mood."

"Where they going?"

"P Street. They got the brilliant idea that it would be really great if they all banged the same hooker. I guess like some kind of initiation or blood brother thing. They're gonna try to squeeze into one taxi and get down there before midnight."

"There's ten of them!"

"Well—eight anyway. They'll make it down there, all right. The question is, will they find a willing whore?"

"How come you're not with them?"

"It's stupid. They're stupid. The whole idea's stupid. I ain't fucking no woman and she's doing it for the money. And I damn sure ain't gonna do it in front of a whole bunch of drunk, hooting assholes. I've got a little something called some morals, you know?"

Culp considered this. "How else you gonna get laid? German girls are hard to come by. Female military is even more rare, and usually ugly."

"True, true. Myself, I say fuck somebody's wife. Somebody's wife is always looking for it. You know?"

"Good moral choice," Culp mumbled.

"What?"

"I said who's that girl there?" Though he was pretty sure.

She was just coming out of the PX, pulling her coat tightly to her thin frame and looking around trying to get her bearings.

Kearns snorted. "Woods' wife. Only like twelve or thirteen years old, little whore from whatever Arkansas shithole they come from. Half the guards at the jail have fucked her."

"Bullshit."

"Bullshit nothing. I know. Even that lezbo guard fucked her before she got transferred out. Believe me, I know."

"You fucked her?"

"Well, no. But I was going to, once. I just couldn't find their house. I got too drunk."

"What? You were just gonna go over there while he's on shift?"

"Well, yeah. What else? You gonna fuck her while he's there? I wouldn't recommend it."

She was walking away, toward the front gate.

"Where's she going? What's her name?"

Kearns shook his head. "Uh uh. No, no, no. C'mon, Culp. What? You're thinking you'll take your turn, huh? Again, I don't recommend it. Carl finds out some guard fucked her, yeah, well, they'll fight, knock each other's teeth out, get drunk together, be best buddies again the next day. He'll slap her around a little. On the other hand of the coin, he finds out *you* fucked her, you're dead. Admin? A counselor? And *his* wife? Man, you are one dead mother. He'll pop a cap in your ass, no shit."

"I'm not getting involved." He watched her turn the corner, heading for the front gate bus stop. "I'm just curious."

"Her name's Lil."

Though it was still summer, the nights and the early mornings were chilly. Culp was double-timing it through the brisk, brightening air from the bus stop toward the front gate of Coleman kaserne. He couldn't afford to be late, ever. The Army takes a dim view of tardiness. He was in civvies and would have to change before formation. Formation was in ten minutes.

Usually there would be a few of the admin platoon gathered around the front door of the barracks, waiting for formation. But not today. The hallway was empty. The whole barracks seemed empty. He got into his fatigues as fast as he could and ran outside. His watch showed 0700 hours, on the dot. No formation. He walked over to the Orderly Room, a sick feeling in the pit of his stomach. He'd missed something, something that would cost him in embarrassment, unforeseeable trouble, or who knows what.

He pushed open the door. At least, someone was there. "What's going on with Admin formation?"

Before the clerk could answer him, the First Sergeant came out of his office. *Have mercy*, Culp thought.

"Culp, you better get on up to the jail. Colonel's having a briefing, wants Counseling staff there. Formation cancelled. Stuart's been up there since early. Get going."

Culp's step was lighter, going up toward the stockade. It gleamed like a city on the hill, sunlight sparkling on the concertina wire, the concrete walls bright in the morning sun. He couldn't be in trouble. He was on time. If there was something going on that changed the schedule on short notice, only those in the barracks, the ones the cadre could reach, were really affected. He stopped at the guard house outside the front gate. To his surprise Sgt. Stuart emerged.

"Ah, Culp, my friend, how good of you to join us of a fine German morning."

"I was on time Sgt. Stuart, I was just—"

"Now now, just relax, nothing's wrong. Staying out all night, though, is not your usual modus operandi, now is it?" Stuart raised his hand. "No, don't tell me where you've been. Remember, I may know more than you think, so don't get caught in a lie. Life lesson, old son: never tell more than is absolutely necessary. Play your cards close to the flak jacket. Keep the lie as close to the truth as possible. You'll have a better chance of remembering what the lie was, exactly."

"I'm not lying."

"And who said you were? Not old Jack. But don't tell me you were at Jessie's, for I called the boy early this a.m., and he was as surprised as I at your nocturnal wanderings."

"I was, uh—"

Stuart smiled. "'He who hesitates is lost'. Never mind. Come on. The Colonel's briefing is about to begin. Something very interesting is going to happen." They entered the compound, walking quickly toward the front door.

"What? What's going to happen?"

"We're getting a new prisoner."

"That's not very interesting. We get twenty new prisoners a week."

"That's not the interesting part."

Culp had only been in the Colonel's office once before. That was when he first arrived. The Colonel had greeted him, welcomed him to the jail, to Germany, etc. It had been an odd meeting of which Culp remembered nothing but his own nervousness and the Colonel's injunction to watch out for German beer. *It's stronger than you imagine*, the Colonel had said.

Stuart held a finger to his lips and eased open the door to the Colonel's office. The room was full. All the guard commanders, their seconds in command, the chaplain, the chaplain's assistant, the mess sergeant, the company commander. Culp could see the other counselors, Dodd, Bennett, Puckett, standing near the windows behind the Colonel's desk. The Colonel towered above his men. He was at least six foot seven, wiry, with a hard look and a gray flat top. His fatigues were starched to a high sheen and pressed into razor-sharp pleats. When he saw Sgt. Stuart had arrived, he began.

"Men, this is our situation. Within the next forty-eight hours, a prisoner will be transferred to this facility from the 22nd MP Group at Stuttgart. He is being held in pre-trial confinement on a seven-year-old desertion charge. According to the CID report I've just read, he deserted his unit in Viet Nam, somehow got out of country, and came to Germany. He may well have fragged his CO in Viet Nam, though that's not clear, and he has not, as of yet, been charged with that crime. According to Interpol reports, when the subject arrived in Germany, he became associated with certain terrorist organizations, notably the Baader-Meinhof gang and the Red Army. Interpol suggests he may have been part of the Maro incident. Army Intelligence, on the other hand, is sure that his connection to the Red Army was marginal. He was probably a member of a small cell away from the central command structure of the organization. But Maro changed everything. Interpol and every national police force cracked down hard, and Baader-Meinhof and the Red Army began major purges. A number of these organizations' members started turning up dead. It is assumed that our subject must have seen the proverbial handwriting on the wall and decided Army jail was better than shot dead and left in the trunk of some car. He turned himself in to the MP station at Vincennes. Had he turned himself into the Italian authorities, he would most certainly be dead by now. He assumes that in our custody he will be safe from his terrorist associates, and, gentlemen, I tell you this now. He is damn-well correct. In here, he will be safer than the President of the United States. I have no idea how long he will be here. I don't think the Judge Advocate General's office has yet decided whether to try him in Germany or in the States. But during this time, there is at least some possibility that an attempt will be made to kill him while he is still in country. And that would mean *in here*. This they will not do. We will house him out of the general population, but otherwise I want him treated like any other prisoner. I don't want any special attention brought to him. I don't want word of who he is to get out among the prisoners nor among the guard platoons, to whatever degree that is possible. I don't want everyone on this kaserne to know we have a high profile prisoner here. Am I making myself clear?" No one said anything. "Then, gentlemen, that is all."

The Colonel held the arms of his chair until he stopped shaking. This prisoner couldn't have come at a better time. His previous command—well, it had gone poorly, though that was not entirely his fault. He'd tried to explain to General Thorpe that two lieutenants under his command had screwed up, but he could hear himself sounding more and more like Captain Queeg with every word out of his mouth. The General had offered him command of the jail. Nobody else wanted it. It was a dead-end. And the General hadn't offered him any other options. He could have resigned his commission. He stood there in the General's office and tried to imagine life back in the world, as a civilian. Forty-two years old, looking for a job after a failed Army career. What would his prospects be? Restaurant manager? Community college teacher? Hardware store clerk?

The Colonel needed something big to happen for him at the jail. He'd made some plans already, but this prisoner was an opportunity unparalleled. The Red Army would come for him. They had to. And the Colonel would be waiting for them.

He held his hand out, palm down, above his desk. The tremor was almost imperceptible. He picked up the phone and called the company commander's office. Of course, there was no way the company commander could have made it back to his office yet. The Colonel left a terse message with the clerk, ordering Lieutenant Mosley to report back to his office immediately with the training schedule for the Guard Platoons. He intended to increase their time on the firing range. Mosley didn't know it, but the Colonel had an old friend from Ft. Benning coming to run things on the range. This friend would be evaluating the guards, looking for the best riflemen in the company. The Colonel wanted a sniper group. As soon as he heard about this prisoner, he starting making the arrangements. He intended to take the best shooters from whatever guard platoons they were on and attach them permanently to the confinement facility. It had never been done before, guard personnel directly under his command.

Yes, he was going to radically reorganize the stockade. He would start by getting rid of the dead wood among the NCOs. Stuart would be the first to go. He could no longer tolerate the man. Stuart's influence was too pervasive. The Colonel had made several calls, trying to get him reassigned, but so far no go. No matter. One way or another, Stuart was history.

The way he saw it, the jail was a dead end only because somebody thought the jail was a dead end. Or because a lot of people thought it was a dead end. But really, that was the only reason. *It was dead end because of a thought.* But nothing real, nothing palpable. Statistics notwithstanding, the future does not have to be like the past. If a fact out there in the world can be constructed from thoughts, then changing people's minds can reconstruct the world. In his favor. He was getting out of this place one way or another.

CHAPTER NINE

18 August 1977, 2100 hours
L'Epi d'Or
Mannheim, Germany

The maitre d' recognized Jessie at once and came forward, greeting him warmly and pressing his hand, finding the expected blue fifty mark note folded neatly therein. He helped Jessie out of his raincoat and led him to a table by the window because, though he did not keep tables empty for his special customers, he remembered Jessie liked the window table, and he was glad it was available and that he could seat him there. And though Jessie always tipped well, he was much more generous when everything was perfect, the food good, the service attentive, the table well-placed.

"Will you to be dining alone this night, sir?" He held the chair and then placed the open napkin in Jessie's lap.

"*Ja*, Karl. *Ein weiss wein, bitte.*" Karl left the menu and scurried away snapping his fingers at a waiter and pointing toward Jessie's table.

Jessie turned toward the window. Rain slicked the glass and the street beyond, falling in mists through the cones of light from the streetlamps. Suddenly he was aware of his reflection staring back at him. Like most of the other men dining at the L'Epi d'Or restaurant, he wore a tuxedo. It was immaculate and recently Omah-pressed. It got little wear. He had, in fact, bought it for the express purpose of coming here. To fit in. L'Epi d'Or was the most expensive and elite French restaurant in Mannheim. There was nothing like it in Heidelberg or Worms. Certainly not in the little village of Lampertheim. One could get in with a nice suit, but to really fit in, a tuxedo was *de rigueur.*

Jessie needed a place like this. He needed a place where a lot of money bought a lot of service but not a lot attention. He needed a place where no one he knew would see him. For no serviceman, at least no enlisted, and probably no officer under the rank of full bird colonel, could get into the L'Epi d'Or. Oh hell, they wouldn't want to anyway. The place was too expensive. It had a dress code. No loud music, no German girls at the bar waiting to meet GIs, no wine-and-Coke cocktails. He tried to imagine Culp trying to get in the front door in his jeans, his Abbey Road tee, and his ragged flannel shirt worn as a jacket. Not that he was avoiding Culp necessarily. No, he needed this place to be alone, to be rich. He had taken a number of precautions to conceal his wealth. In truth, only Stuart knew just how much money he had.

That had been a weird day. First the telegram telling him his grandfather had died. Then the call from the attorney. Boyd Lamar had had a hell of a time getting hold of Jessie. The phones on military kasernes in Germany were on the same lines strung up by the Third Reich, and getting through from base to base was problematic. Trying to call somebody out on the regular German phone system could take hours. But calling overseas—well, somehow the lawyer had gotten through. Lamar had insisted on arranging an immediate discharge and Jessie's return to the States. Oh, he had it all worked out. He had wanted Jessie to authorize him fifty thousand dollars and a limited power of attorney, and he would handle everything related to getting him out of the military and into his grandfather's offices. The congressman from Jessie's home district would ask the Army for a hardship discharge, given Jessie's recent familial loss. It was all completely legal, of course. The money would just make things go more smoothly. The power of attorney, well, the power of attorney would simply provide the lawyer the means to have the will probated while Jessie was getting discharged.

It had all been very tempting. Jessie hated the Army. He hated the jail. He had sometimes thought that being dead would be better. To just turn and walk away from all of the *bullshit*! But Jessie didn't even know this man, this Boyd Lamar. He had been his grandfather's attorney. He was not Jessie's attorney, at least not yet. There was simply no way to know if the man had Jessie's best interests at heart. Jessie thought for a long minute about the idea of *lawyer's ethics*, and decided not to sign any power of attorney.

Instead, he told Lamar him to wire five thousand dollars and asked about the old man's funeral arrangements. Those had been prepared for in his grandfather's will. But no accommodation had been made for the sole heir to get there from Germany on short notice. Jessie had three days to make the funeral.

Stuart took care of the leave. The first sergeant grunted and groused, trying to make things hard, but Stuart had stepped in, told the first sergeant that Jessie was getting an emergency hardship leave and that would be the end of it. Stuart also drove him to Frankfurt to catch the plane. He was puzzled about Jessie paying good money for a civilian flight when Stuart could have gotten him on a military transport with ease. And for nothing. Jessie thought he could trust Stuart, but still he didn't tell him about the money. What he told Stuart was that he just couldn't deal with any military crap, and though the look on Stuart's face betrayed his doubt, Stuart asked no more about it.

Stuart would have been even more suspicious had he known that, in fact, Jessie was flying first class. He changed into civilian clothes in the airport bathroom after Stuart left. It felt good to be a civilian again. The stewardesses were markedly different in first class. One young and very cute one stood by his seat, her knee propped on the armrest, asking him about his trip and swaying back and forth in sort of a shy, little girl way. She gave him a card with a phone number on it and said she'd be in Memphis three days if he wanted to call her. Eighteen months in the Army and no woman had even looked at him twice, and now out of uniform ten hours and a beautiful stewardess wanted him to call her. He'd heard it many times before and now he believed it: *the Army could fuck up a wet dream.*

Jessie's parents had been killed when he was nine. They died in a plane crash somewhere in Mexico, on some vacation without him. Many times he had wondered why they left him in his grandfather's care, why they hadn't arranged for him to live with some godparents or something. True, his father had been an only child, just like him. And if his mother had brothers, sisters, parents still alive somewhere, well, they had never tried to contact him after his parents' deaths. Maybe there was just no one but his grandfather left to take over his rearing. *I mean, surely they wouldn't have left me with Grandfather on purpose. They couldn't have been that cruel.* Unless, of course, they had simply never seen the old man the way he had. That was at least possible, he supposed. But, probably, yes, much more probably, they had just never expected to die so young.

So Jessie had grown up in his grandfather's house. And a strange house it was too. It sat on a tiny rectangle of grass behind a high ornate fence that seemed to be made of spears standing upright, just at the edge of downtown Memphis. The front of the house faced downtown, tall buildings, clean concrete and glass rising toward the clouds. Behind the house, right up to the back of the fence in fact, were the poor houses of the poorest blacks in Memphis, an area known as Sugartown. The house was like some dividing point between the commerce and the money of the city and the moneyless, ignored black populace on whose backs the city had been built.

Well, if not the whole city, then at least this house. It was a rectangular brick monolith, like a short chimney sticking out of the ground. Red brick and mortar, two stories, though not really large. There were only two windows, both upstairs, one in his bedroom and one in the old man's. They were small, you couldn't climb out of them, though that clearly was not why: no one could climb into them either. The old man owned, in addition to several blocks of downtown Memphis for which he received huge rents, most of the slum houses that abutted downtown. Jessie had never thought much about it until he turned eighteen. That was when the old man had said he wanted Jessie to take over collections in Sugartown. He was supposed to go door to door on the first five days of every month trying to collect the rents from the people who occupied the houses there. Most of the houses were shotgun shacks badly in need of repair. He usually started about five-thirty in the afternoon when the people were coming home from work, and he collected until about ten. Collecting, or trying to collect, was bad enough. But then he and the old man stayed up most of the night counting the money and keeping tabs on who was paid up and who was behind in their rent. The bills were dirty and old and almost black, greasy to the touch. The old man and Jessie stacked little piles of the take all over the dining room table. And the old man gave him hell about not collecting all the rents. *No excuses!* the old man would shout. *Those worthless niggers will lie to you in a New York minute. You've got to be tough. Threaten them. Throw them out.* It was pretty clear to Jessie that the old man wished he could still be going down there himself to do the collecting.

One night walking back toward the house through Sugartown, a car passed him, and he heard someone mutter, "Mistuh Landlord," and it occurred to him for the first time that he ought to be scared walking around there at night. With rent money in his pockets. It had never occurred to him before. As a teenager he'd walked through Sugartown regularly, invisibly, he'd assumed. Now he realized he was the most visible person in Sugartown. Had been, all his life.

And then, approaching his grandfather's house from the rear, he saw that it was not a rich man's house. It was a prison. It was a prison-fortress. Built for only one reason. To protect the old man in his paranoia from the people he exploited. Built against the day, though it hadn't come yet and probably wouldn't in his lifetime, when the blacks rose up, not satisfied any longer with simple justice, but thirsty for revenge. And the old man believed himself safe behind his fence, in his brick fortress, no ground floor windows, solid steel front door.

And then stopping in front of the house and looking at the lights of Memphis, Jessie had an insight, an epiphany so full and so real that it literally shook him from head to toe. The old man must make ten times, hundreds of times more money from his downtown properties than from the poor rent shacks he owned in Sugartown. So why did he keep them? Why did he stay up all night accounting for the money, indeed accounting for the lives of those people behind his house? Jessie had never heard him mention any other business besides Sugartown. He had construction going on all the time downtown. Parking lots, new buildings, renovations. Never mentioned them. Because why?

The next day Jessie joined the Army, asked to be sent as far away from Memphis as possible. He left a note for the old man. They'd never been close. Never really talked all that much until he started collecting rents. And then only complaints. None of his school friends ever wanted to come over to his house, and once they did, they never came back. He didn't even pack anything. Went with the clothes he had on. Was in South Carolina in Basic Training within a week. Never looked back.

At least not until the old man died.

Jessie had to rush straight from the airport to the cemetery. The old man's lawyer sent a limo to pick him up. The driver dropped him near the plot, helped him shoulder into a black trench coat, and handed him an umbrella. A heavy mist fell on a lush, greeny gray cemetery from a uniformly gray sky. There were fewer than ten people at the graveside. Most of them were probably lawyers and accountants, there to impress him. He saw Eva May, the old man's black housekeeper. When the minister finished, Jessie asked Boyd Lamar what arrangements the old man had made for her in his will. The lawyer said no provision whatsoever had been made for her.

"I want you to retire her," Jessie said.

"She's already been fired, if that's what you mean," Lamar said.

Jessie turned on him. "That sure the fuck isn't what I meant."

The man flushed. "I'm sorry, I thought—"

"That woman practically raised me. Fuck!" Jessie walked away and stared off into the sky for a moment. Lamar trailed behind. Then Jessie turned to him and said, "Okay, here's what you're going do. First thing, phony up some paperwork, have her sign it, and tell her, I don't know, tell her that she's earned her pension. And then start paying her, oh, let's say, three times what she made from my grandfather. Hm. What else? Oh, then tell her that when she dies, ten years worth of her salary will go to her heirs. Tell her it's her 'inheritance' or some such. In fact, have a will made up and ready for her to sign while she's there. Put money into a trust to take care of all of that, you know, the retirement checks and the inheritance. Okay, what else, what else?"

Lamar cleared his throat. "Sir, I don't think your grandfather would—"

"No, I know. Let's send somebody out to see what her house looks like, if it needs any repairs, roof, plumbing, whatever. And, you know what? If necessary, just buy another house, put it in her name, and move her in. And," Jessie turned his back on Lamar, "don't say one more fucking word to me until we're in your office."

As the old man was lowered into the ground by hydraulic lift, Jessie felt the power of the money descend upon him like the mist falling all around, soaking the mourners, such as they were. He hugged Eva May and told her that the limo would take her home. "Wait here just a minute, please. I have to talk to this man. Then we'll get you home." He walked back to where Lamar was still waiting by the grave and said, said, "Give me your car keys."

The man looked startled.

"Not a fucking word. Just give me your keys and point out which car it is." Lamar complied, sputtering, looking around for support from his yes-men, all of whom were shifting from foot to foot, staring at the wet ground. "I'm going to check into a hotel. I will meet you at your office at ten o'clock tomorrow morning to go over the will, and at that time I will tell you how the estate is to be handled, and I will let you know then if, and I repeat if, you and your firm will have any stake in the future handling of my grandfather's properties. Clear enough?"

Lamar opened his mouth, shut it just as quickly, and nodded.

And with that Jessie turned away and walked Eva May to the limo that had brought him. He told the driver to take her wherever she wanted to go for the rest of the day. When she was in the back of the car, Jessie put a finger on the driver's chest and told him to treat her with the utmost respect and to be sure she got home. As they pulled away, she turned her sad face toward the rear window and stared at him until the car disappeared around a curve. The ground was soft under his feet, there was water in his shoes, and he felt he might sink into the earth where the old man now lay down for the last time.

CHAPTER TEN

2 September 1977, 0320 hours
U.S. Army Area Confinement Facility
Coleman Kaserne
Mannheim, Germany

The windowless van pulled up in front of Gate One at 0320 hours. PFC Carole Kelly stepped out of the gatehouse and stared down the driver who was already showing her his clipboard, trying to unload his cargo and get going as soon as possible. Just another prisoner drop, nothing unusual. But Kelly was having none of it. She started giving the driver no end of shit—the paperwork was wrong, what did he mean bringing in a prisoner at this hour, where was the prisoner's personal property report form? All stuff she knew he didn't know, couldn't know. The MP riding shotgun got out and came around to take sides with the driver, but she bullied him into a meek submission that would have made Sgt. Stuart proud, if only he were still her platoon sergeant. *If only!* She'd be inside tonight, that's for sure. Chivalry was not a dead art to Stuart, she thought.

"Leave him cuffed, numb nuts," she barked at the MP pulling the prisoner out of the back of the van.

"I was just gonna cuff him behind his back, geez. Isn't that the way you guys like it." The MP's hair was cut very short. She could see the sides of his head shining between his ears and his cap. He'd emphasized *guys* and *like it* in a way that suggested something sexual, something designed to be both insulting and invitational.

She stepped up nose to nose with him. To his credit, he didn't back up an inch. Didn't even flinch. "I'm not a guy. And in a hundred years you couldn't figure out how I *like it*."

He snorted. "Take a pill."

She ordered the prisoner to stand in front of the gate. She took the keys from the MP and uncuffed the prisoner. Then she whipped out another pair of cuffs, pushed him against the fence mesh of the gate, and cuffed him behind his back. *Why doesn't his uniform have any rank or insignia?* No unit patches, no name tag, like it was a new uniform off the rack. She stood him off to the side and turned to the MP, dangling his cuffs from her middle finger.

"Not going to leave without these, were you, General?"

As the van pulled away beneath the floodlights in the stockade parking lot, Kelly watched both driver and MP salute her with the finger. She chuckled to herself. It was too bad really. She could have gone for that MP. Something about those white sidewalls. But in front of a prisoner, she never let down. If she were in any way soft, the prisoner might think he could get over on her, mouth off, wheedle her for cigarettes, hell, even try to knock her down and run for it. She stepped just inside the door of the gatehouse and called inside for someone to come get him. She'd have to get a look at this guy's paperwork, maybe find out where that MP was stationed.

Lee tried to wiggle his hands around a bit. This stockade guard had put the handcuffs on much tighter than the MPs back at Heidelberg. Now she was in the gatehouse, shuffling through the papers the driver had given her. Every now and again she glanced up to see if he was still there. Not worried though, perhaps daring him to run for it. Not that he would. Well, if she read enough of the paperwork and had the where-withal, she'd soon know why.

The enormous front door of the stockade opened, throwing a bright light onto him, the fence, the yard, the gatehouse so suddenly *there*, and two guards came down the steps toward the front gate. Lee glanced at them and quickly dropped his gaze. A tall one with a fat young face and a short one, undistinguished. He didn't need to know more. Hell, he didn't need to know that much. Certainly he didn't want to make eye contact, stand out, be noticed. One of them grabbed his arm and moved him inside the gate. Then the great door swung closed plunging the small stage of his second incarceration in a week into darkness, and both men went inside the gatehouse with the female guard. He couldn't hear what they were saying, only the rumble of their voices, and then just before they came back out he heard the woman yell *Fuck off*, and they came out and took him through the big door into the confinement facility.

Just inside the large door was what might under other circumstances be called a foyer. It was a receiving area, for there was another large gate opposite the one he'd just come through, and it seemed clear that that way lead to the jail proper. There was a bench against one wall, though he was not invited to sit. The opposite wall was much like a row of bank teller windows with thick glass from the ceiling down to counter. He stood at attention before the glass, behind which guards of various low rank peeked around papers, openly stared, or ignored him altogether. The guards who'd escorted him in were in a heated, but low toned, dispute over something. Apparently the sergeant of the guard was unavailable to do something. The discussion became more heated. At that precise moment something seemed to shift in his vision, and he felt at a remove from himself, a cliché he'd heard often enough, *I felt outside of myself*, some fool would say, after shooting someone or demolishing some structure and the bodies of people with a bomb, a cliché now very real, as real as pain, abject fear transforming the subjective to the objective. Making him babble, the surface of his stream of consciousness a delicious, cold menu of objective word choices, precise incoherence, driving him farther and farther out of his body, wondering if his loss of proximity, his loss of the heavy bear, would turn the subjective him into an hysterical crying animal while his higher self, his Transparent Eyeball, was removed, observing, glossing, unable to shut up, to turn off the stream of words, stop, stop, stop, fear is the only enemy, my mantra, fear is the mind-killer, the little death that brings total obliteration, fear—

"OPEN the GOD damn GATE!"

The shout from this side of the glass echoed in the empty foyer and knocked Lee out of his reverie and back into his body. The reality of his reunification was aptly demonstrated when the big, baby faced one yanked him by the shoulder of his field jacket up to the glass and said, "This prisoner is a security risk." Baby Face was calming down. "He's supposed to be in D Block. I need to get him out of general population quick," he said more quietly.

"He's not in gen pop, Carl, he's right here, with us." This from a painfully thin PFC, with a bad case of acne, who was probably being overzealous in his duty, maybe his first time in such an important position: who gets in, who stays out.

"I don't know the nature of the beast here, Milton, but if something happens to him it's my ass. Then it's your ass. Then it's everybody's ass." Baby Face gave Acne a look that was supposed to be significant, loaded with hidden meaning and with hidden threat. "And finally, it'll be Sgt. Chambers' ass. I'm sure you want to be responsible for that."

But clearly Acne did *not* want to be responsible for that. He moved to his left a bit and touched something underneath the counter that popped open the huge inside gate with a loud clang. Baby Face dragged Lee by the jacket through the gate and down a gray hall, gray floor, gray walls, gray ceiling, gray doors, and then through one of the doors.

Only one of the ceiling lights was on in the small room. The one window was pushed open and the bars were silhouetted against the first pink ribbons of light climbing in the east. There were a table and two chairs. Nothing else. The short guard removed the handcuffs and Lee rubbed his wrists, hoping he might be told to sit down.

Instead Baby Face told him to strip.

Carl watched the prisoner. The son-of-a-bitch was slow as Christmas. Folding his pants so perfectly. Carl resisted the urge, so strong, to knock him to the floor. Thornton, the little weasel, leaned against the wall. A shit, a weakling, a coward, but one who knew how to keep his mouth shut. He had known about Watson. And he kept shut up about that.

He'd watched Carl twist the sheet around the nigger's neck till his tongue slid out and turned blue, and he'd helped Carl tie him to the bars in the cell. And he had kept his mouth shut. He looked up to Carl, knew him to be a man with a capital M. Jesus, compared to the fucks that buzzed around Woods like flies, that followed him to P Street or to the gasthaus, he was Superman. The little nigger had cussed Carl out and then—*then!*—turned his back on him.

And now, as then, as the day Carl had killed Watson and found himself beyond all that shit like right and wrong, a sour stink seemed to rise from the floor, the reek of a dead thing, and now, as then, something fluttered like dark birds in the corners of the room. And now he saw a mossy hand reach up from outside and grab hold of one of the window bars.

And so it spoke again. One word, something German, something that sounded like *mocked*, but felt like a spoon punched handle first into his gut. His face burned and he could feel a vein somewhere inside his head pounding, pounding to bust out the front of his skull. Then he made himself move. He'd been planning it a while so he was ready. Killing Watson had scared him. Then it freed him. He could do whatever he wanted. And he had a whole prison full of scumbags and maggots to do it to. The world had lost sight of how great a thing killing was. Now guns made every wimp and weakling a murderer. But to kill with your hands. That made you a man among ants, a god among children.

Thornton was going through the prisoner's clothes. Not that Carl cared, but there was nothing there. No papers, no cigarettes, no money. Didn't matter. Carl stepped up very close to the prisoner and looked into his eyes. He wouldn't look up, so Carl reached out and took hold of the prisoner's balls. His eyes snapped up then. He looked afraid. It was a look that made Carl hard. He felt the man's balls tighten up, and he held them firm but without squeezing, not hurting him, but—what?

Now Thornton was looking at them with his big stupid mouth open. He stammered something, but couldn't make words. Carl turned the prisoner around and cuffed his hands behind him. He picked up the man's issue boxers—who the fuck wore these after Basic?—and punched him very hard in the stomach. Lee fell over the table and Carl pushed the shorts into his gasping mouth.

"Hold him down," he told Thornton, who came over and leaned on the prisoner's back. Then Carl walked around to where the prisoner's face was pressed against the table and dropped his pants. His cock was hard, a brick hard any man would be proud of, any real man, and he let it sway there in front of the prisoner's face. Let him get a good look at it. He let some spit drop in a long strand onto the head and he smeared it around. The man squeezed his eyes shut and Carl wondered what it would be like to staple them open. He leaned down and whispered into the man's ear, but loud enough for Thornton to hear too.

"In here, I'm Death. And I'm going to fuck you one way or the other." He looked up at the rabbitfied eyes of his pitiful helper and said, "Maybe both."

Lee had made a sort of a religion of dignity. He admired it in others, and he loved it in himself. He had found a kind of dignity in the Army, of all places, in Basic Training, where his drill sergeant, Sgt. Alexander Brody, a man to whom Lee still looked up, had taught the new recruits how to become soldiers, which he told them would take a while, and how to pretend to be soldiers in the interim. While in the battalions and brigades and companies around them, even in the other platoons within their own company, drill sergeants bullied, beat, and tried to break their charges down so they could have a blank slate upon which to build soldiers who followed orders, Sgt. Brody balanced their training between a nearly fatal physical regime and a symposium in the philosophy of soldiering and the art of war.

In Lee's advanced training, Sgt. Brody's teachings had served him well. When he'd asked for Engineers, he thought he'd be building bridges. He found himself instead being trained to blast them into tiny, useless pieces, and this he did, and did well, and it made him proud. His pride gave him dignity, his dignity gave him calm, and his calm made him the best demolitions man in his class. He didn't enjoy the work, but he enjoyed doing it well and being the best at it. Crouched in a ditch with an instructor and another trainee while the other trainee tried to arm a trip wire with trembling hands and perspiration dripping into his eyes, Lee could keep his calm. Some of the trainees accidently detonated their devices while setting them, killing themselves, their comrades, and their instructors. Fear, he learned, can demolish knowledge and training and common sense as surely as plastique can demolish a column of soldiers. And the greater the fear—the more one has on the line—the less presence of mind one has to work with. More than once he'd saved his own life and others, simply reaching out to stop a false move or steady a shaking hand. Once an instructor had thanked him afterward. "I saw what he was gonna do, but I couldn't make myself move. He'd have killed us." That trainee had run many punishment miles, pushed many punishment pushups, but Lee always suspected he managed to blow himself up somewhere later. Lee finished first in the class. First in destruction.

But Viet Nam changed everything. In Viet Nam he discovered no pride. He found no dignity. From what he heard, there was some real soldiering going on in other places in country. But not in his company. Not under his lieutenant. Lee had been called upon to destroy objectives he clearly recognized as civilian. He had, in fact, been called upon to demolish civilians. And he had done so. He had done so until he could no longer stand it. Then one night he detonated a small incendiary device under the hootch of his company commander, a man he hated with a white-hot intensity that burned like phosphorous in his stomach, though now he couldn't quite remember the man's name. Kowalski? Kolodney? No matter now. He had watched the man stagger out of the small inferno and flop grotesquely on the ground for a minute or two. Then he was still. Several soldiers tried to put out the fire that was their former commander, but to no avail. Eventually they would have gotten around to asking him how to put the fire out, he suspected, but by then he was gone. He went AWOL. He deserted. He didn't look back. That was seven years ago.

Getting out of the Republic of Viet Nam was easier than he thought it would be. It was his intention to join the Other Side, whoever they might be. The VC were out of the question. They would have killed him before he could explain his disenchantment and defection, even if they believed him. He planned to work his way back to the States and join the anti-war movement, the underground of Abbie Hoffman and Huey Newton, but he'd never gotten that far. He got as far as Italy, by way of Turkey, and found himself sitting at a bar next to an Italian who'd gone to the University of Chicago, where Lee's parents taught and where he himself had attended one year before being drafted. Their talk of Chicago, the university, his parents and their arm-chair Communism, and his red-diaper upbringing led to the revelation that the man, Paolo Prevost, was a member of the radical Red Army, a group dedicated to bringing revolutionary change to Italy by any means necessary. Specifically, violent change.

And Lee found a home with them. Not at first, of course. Paolo was naturally suspicious when Lee told him of his Army days, his training in demolitions, and his desertion. Lee left out any mention of fragging his company commander. But Paola did take him home with him. The Red Army had enough intelligence capability to check out him and his story. When Paolo took him to meet the leaders of his cell, they were able to tell him things he didn't know. For instance, that he was suspected in the death of his CO, but there was no real evidence, and that he'd only been charged with desertion so far. They indicated they were sure he'd killed the lieutenant and that as far as they were concerned that was all the resume he needed to join them if he wished. That he was a "demolitions expert" did not impress them. They were all hands-on demolitions experts, they said—which he took to be some kind of an explosives joke—and they would re-teach him about the chemicals they worked with and about their procedures. This they did.

It had been an interesting seven years. He'd traveled all over Europe blowing things to kingdom come. It turned out that the Red Army had more than a passing acquaintance with the Baader-Meinhof group from West Germany and that they conducted many operations jointly. He'd enjoyed the Germans more so than the Italians, but probably because more of them spoke English, and his German was better than his Italian. If he'd expected the rant and roar of political sermonizing, well, there was some, but in truth the philosophers were few, and the ones who could talk intelligently weren't often in the mood. Actually, he was surprised that most of the soldiers were no better than grown children, bullies knocking over other children's blocks, kicking down their sandcastles, yanking down their pants. They could carelessly murder and mutilate, without emotion or affect, yet they were capable of great loyalty, to family and to anyone in the movement, and heedlessly uncritical of major personality and psychological faults in their brothers and sisters in the struggle. They also enjoyed the money.

They were well-financed. Lee was never sure from where. The brigade commanders talked knowingly of instructions, and monies, from Moscow or Peking or Havana, but Lee never found them believable. They were too earnest, too rehearsed. But maybe not. Maybe they *were* believable. Maybe Lee had simply forgotten how to believe people. And why. He'd never made any friends among soldiers with whom he'd spent the last seven years. Well, he was sure many of them thought of *him* as a friend, but he never felt the kind of mutual trust and loyalty he associated with friends rather than acquaintances. Was it possible that the whole Moro thing was just a pathological lack of trust on his part? A bright blinding flash of paranoia? No, he stuck by his intuition that if one were able to self-diagnose any mental abnormality, that fact was evidence enough to prove the contrary. And even if he was paranoid, that didn't mean the brigade commanders *weren't* planning to kill every perceived weak link in the cells. And then probably anyone else they disliked. Lee, for instance.

But that was all moot now. He had run. He had taken nothing except what he was wearing when Eric had offered his opinion that if he were in charge, he'd kill everyone below the rank of brigade commander, clean out the bank accounts, and lie low until Moro blew over. So Lee had run—straight into the arms of Uncle Sam. He could conceivably spend the rest of his life in jail. Then again, he might not. The right lawyer, one of his parents' high powered, liberal friends, might find a way to get him out much sooner. Either way it would all happen in the States, far away from the Red Army's considerable reach. Even here, in the custody of the U.S. Army, he felt out of danger.

Well, not completely, he supposed. Baby Face was standing behind Lee, spitting, it seemed, down the crack of his behind. Then he positioned himself, sort of hunkered down over Lee's back, and pushed it in.

Both men groaned. Beyond the pain and fear and humiliation, Lee's mind was again strangely detached, and he thought of something he'd read somewhere that the sounds of sexual pleasure and physical pain were so similar as to be nearly indistinguishable. Where had he read that? Sade? *The Story of O?* The little guy was pressed against the wall as if he were trying to disappear into it. The sensation of the man's penis in him was unpleasant, as if his bowels were very full and he needed to evacuate them, or were in the process of a painful defecation. Worse was the table pressed into his midsection and the weight of Baby Face on him. Baby Face grabbed hold of the back of his head by the hair and smacked Lee's forehead against the table as he came. The blow made Lee dizzy. The most intense pain, though, came at the end when the man yanked his cock out. He continued to hold Lee down on the table as he exhorted the other man to take his turn.

Lee could feel the first man's semen running out and down his legs. He tried to get up, but the big man pushed him down hard, and told the other man to hurry. And indeed, the little man dropped his pants and stepped up behind Lee. But, for whatever reason, the man could not get an erection and just pushed his flaccid penis against Lee's buttocks until Baby Face pulled him off and berated and mocked him for his impotence. Then Baby Face ordered the man to remove Lee's handcuffs and leave the room.

When Lee turned around the big man was standing there slapping a long nightstick or billy club into his hand, in some pathetic parody of the cop on the beat. Lee wondered what was expected of him now. His clothes were on the floor, and he began to put them on. Should he lunge at the man and attempt to revenge the sodomy? Was his passive acceptance of the act a sign of his weakness? Should he take a beating from the man to prove he was no pushover? He nearly laughed aloud at his own pun. But Lee got the distinct impression that the man wanted him to attack. That was the point of the club, to guarantee victory. When he finished dressing, he sat down in the chair.

"I need a cigarette," Baby Face said. "How about you?" And laughed at his pathetic joke.

Lee thought he might need to vomit, but didn't say so.

CHAPTER ELEVEN

22 September 1977, 1800 hours
Coleman Kaserne

Culp could never be sure what to believe. The stockade buzzed with rumors and lies and wild stories. He was more afraid of the guards than the prisoners. The guards accused the counselors of coddling the prisoners. Culp had tried to explain to a couple a guards once that their job was to incarcerate the prisoners, to hold them, not to add to their punishment with humiliation and degradation and intimidation. They had been walking to the stockade from the barracks. The guards told him he was a fucking pussy and one of them knocked him down. They walked away laughing.

Culp shared a two-room office with three other counselors, Dodd, Bennett and Puckett. Until just two months before, there had been eight counselors, and now the case load was out of control. At the moment Culp was lying on the floor next to his desk. Bennett looked at him and shook his head. It was almost time to leave.

"Get up, you idiot. That floor is filthy."

Culp looked around. The floor was ridiculously clean. Surreally clean. He sat up and watched Dodd pack his briefcase. Dodd actually took work home with him. The other counselors were trudging out of the office. Every desk was piled with bulging folders, unfinished paperwork, unanswered mail, notes from prisoners: *call my lawyer, can I see the Colonel, help me, help me.* The walls were hung with calendars, schedules, memoranda, lists of mandatory briefings, drills, formations and classes. Every day was a long one, and he was glad this one was over.

Between the office and the parking lot Culp had to pass six floor-to-ceiling gray-barred gates. The guards standing post at these gates unlocked them with large brass keys. The last one was opened electronically by a guard behind a huge bulletproof glass window. It was conventional that as you approached the gate, you would call out "Gate!" and the guard would push the buzzer to release the gate. Most guards timed it perfectly. The buzzer sounded the instant you reached out your hand for it. It was like opening any door. Not today.

Culp was standing before the gate, but no buzzer. Sometimes they were busy. Putting away a file. Getting off the phone. A few seconds at most. Not today.

He knew what the guard wanted. He wanted Culp to look at him, to ask him with that look, *let me out please.* In his two months here, he had looked before, at first from mystification, then from irritation. But now he didn't look anymore. He had decided that he would stand here until they opened it, no matter how long that was. He knew the guard was looking at him. He could feel the stare. The side of his face felt warm, and he was acutely aware of his peripheral vision. He could imagine himself standing here until he died, until he dried up and was scattered down the hall, to be swept up by the prisoners. They did keep a nice hall.

He lost track of time. How long had he been standing there? He could imagine the guard's face. His grin. Culp wasn't going to turn and look. Maybe he was nudging another guard. And they were both just staring at him. Burning him down with their eyes. Culp heard boots down the hall. The buzzer sounded. Culp turned his head and saw the Colonel coming. The buzzer stopped. The Colonel passed his office and continued toward Culp, his head down, reading something in a file. He walked up and stood next to Culp without looking at him. The guard behind the glass must have lost it. He didn't push the buzzer again. The Colonel looked up.

"What's the problem?" he said.

Culp shrugged.

The Colonel looked past Culp at the guard. Now the buzzer sounded and Culp pushed through. He glanced over his shoulder and saw the Colonel walk over to the glass partition. The buzzer to let Culp out the second gate, the outside gate, buzzed right on time, but Culp could hear the Colonel asking the guard what was going on with the gate. Culp didn't wait to hear the answer.

It was nearly dark. The western sky was bruised violet and yellow. The path from the jail to the barracks led through a wide shallow gully. The guards had built a firing range within earshot of the stockade. Culp passed the place where the guard had knocked him down. As he climbed the path out of the gully he saw a man standing off the side of the path. Culp saw the orange glow of the man's cigarette and then the trail of sparks when he snapped it away into the bushes. The man stepped onto the path blocking Culp's way.

"Do you work at the stockade?" His accent was thick. And he was wearing a leather suit. Green.

"No," Culp said, "just visiting a buddy." Culp stepped around the man and walked quickly toward the lights of the barracks.

"I have a friend there too," the man called after him. Culp did not turn around.

Because of the rotating shifts they had to work, guards were always roaming the noisy hallways of the barracks, some starting their workdays at 2300 hours, cheerful and carefully groomed; others getting off work, drunk and belligerent by midnight. Country, soul, and rock music competed night and day at top volume on state-of-the-art German stereo equipment.

The other counselors lived off post with their wives. When Culp entered his barracks room, his roommates, Wilson and Williams, were circling each other in the middle of the room, looking each other up and down like fighters in the ring. They wore four-inch platform shoes, crazy disco shirts, and flared pants.

"Hey, Cup! You hear they caught a Baader-Meinhof?" Williams said.

"What?" Culp said.

"Cup don't care about that shit," Wilson, making a slick little turn and clapping his hands in Culp's face.

Williams said, "They caught this radical terrorist type guy from the Baader-Meinhofs and they're bringing him right here to our little old jailhouse, man. And—his buddies from the BM are 'sposed to be coming to break him out or snuff him or some shit."

"Where'd you hear that?" Culp said.

"From yo lady love in the Orderly Room," Wilson whispered in a little sing song voice.

"She's not my—"

"Give it up, Cup!" Wilson said. "She's warm for yo form, man. Oh yeah. Sure she's a booger eating moron, but she's all about you, and you fucking knows it!" Wilson was shouting.

"Give it a rest, bro," Williams said. "Cup ain't studying that shit. Hey, Cup, come on out with us tonight. We're going over to the Eichbaum on the other side of Mannheim. Many juicy frauleins up in there."

"Shee-it," Wilson said. "Cup ain't been outta the barracks since he got here that I'm aware of.

"I'm not feeling too good," Culp said.

"See. What'd I say? He ain't coming. Hell, home, do you really want him to. Damn tub of lard." Wilson was changing into different garish paisley shirt.

"Do you good, Cup. Sure you won't come?" Williams was heading toward the door.

"I'm just gonna hang out." Culp rolled over and closed his eyes.

When Wilson and Williams returned much later that night, they were drunk and loud. Culp woke and lay in the dark listening to them trying to whisper and giggling and shushing each other. They settled into their bunks and were soon snoring. Culp thought about Lil. It was ridiculous, of course. She was Woods' wife. And Woods was the craziest of the crazy shit house rats that composed the most violent group of guards at the jail: First Platoon. There were a lot of stories about him. Culp had seen him reeling drunk up and down the barracks halls even though he lived out on the economy. He'd fight any guard from any platoon. Culp had watched from an upstairs window while Woods nearly beat the life out of that red-headed guy from Third Platoon. Woods' friends had to pull him off the unconscious man whom Woods was still beating. But one night, drinking the local beer in the barracks room, Wilson and Williams had told him a story about Woods getting so mad at a prisoner that he choked him to death and hung him up with a sheet to make it look like suicide. Wilson had laughed as he described the prisoner getting in Woods' face, cursing him and spitting in his face. Then Woods grabbing him by the throat and picking him up off the ground and holding him up until he was dead. Williams said that Stuart had covered it up, covered everything up, sold the suicide story to the Captain, to the Colonel, to the CID. Said Woods went back to work and nothing was ever said. Williams and Wilson cursed Stuart, he shoulda turned that crazy fucker over to CID, put his racist ass on a plane to Leavenworth, locked the psycho son of a bitch up for the rest of his miserable life. They turned their puzzled eyes to Culp. Yes, Culp was Stuart's boy, but he couldn't understand why Stuart had protected Woods anymore than they could. *And if it came down to a choice between Woods and Culp, who would Stuart protect?*

Culp got up and got dressed in the dark. He walked through the company streets to the front gate of the kaserne. The guards at the front gate stopped him and asked him where he was going. "You're supposed to stop me coming in, not going out," Culp said.

They looked at his field jacket. "You work at the Stockade? Go on, then. Just be sure to get back in time for formation."

"I'm off tomorrow," Culp told them, but they had already gone back into the guard shack. *Just looking out for me*, he thought. *I probably need it.* He walked to the bus stop and waited for the bus that would take him toward Donner strasse.

The bus was stinky and stuffy. Culp sat near the front and looked at the city. Donner strasse was on the other side of town. There was not a single person on the streets. Then again, it was 0400. The streetlights and business signs were bluish and the concrete and glass glowed like a city on an alien planet. A crazy dark planet. Maybe that weird planet in *A Wrinkle in Time* where that giant brain was in charge. He might as well be on another planet for all the connection he felt in this country, at the jail, in his job, in the barracks.

The only place he'd felt anything like happy since he got here was Jessie's house. Stuart had taken him there last weekend. Jessie seemed a little put out when he saw Culp, but he warmed up and made Culp feel at home. Jessie's house was like being back in the world. Lots of food and beer, books on the shelves, good music on a great stereo. American girls, real cocolas, black hash. Jessie lived in the top floor of a huge house out in some little village south of Mannheim. Culp ate a couple of really good ham sandwiches and drank some beers. He sat in a circle of people passing a hash pipe, but none of them talked to him, so he looked around for Stuart. He was engrossed in talking to a blond woman with huge breasts and the tiniest waist Culp had ever seen. Jessie was nowhere to be found. Culp stepped out onto a little balcony and looked out over the lights of the village. Jessie came out a few minutes later, looked surprised to see him, then pulled up a chair and propped his feet on the railing.

"How've you been, Byron? Stuart taking good care of you?"

"I hate the fucking jail. I hate the fucking guards. Everybody in the barracks is an asshole. If there's a non-asshole somewhere, then he must think I'm an asshole cause he's avoiding me like the plague. I don't know anybody. I go to work, I go to eat, I go to the barracks and wait to go to bed."

"You need a life, old son," Jessie said. He churchkeyed a beer open and flipped the key into a potted plant.

Culp looked over his shoulder into the house and then at Jessie. "There is no life for me. A good life of any kind is going to cost money. I'm stuck in the barracks. Hell, there's three guys from Admin platoon sharing in a two-room roach coach somewhere in Mannheim, starving to death trying to pay the rent, just to get away from the guards." *How do you afford all this?* Culp thought.

Jessie said nothing. A soft wind blew river smells across them and through the village. The streets were empty. Every window cover was drawn, not a light visible in any house.

Stuart stuck his head out of the door. "Let's go, Culp. I told what's-his-name I'd have his car back at the barracks by two. So long, Jessie. See you in the movies."

Culp got up. "Thanks for inviting me over. See you around." Jessie didn't respond. It had occurred to Culp then that maybe Jessie was among those who thought he was an asshole.

Now the bus turned onto a street Culp recognized as the one that crossed Donner strasse. He got up and went to the front of the bus. In a moment he said, "*Hier, bitte.*"

The bus stopped and Culp stepped down into the chilly dark. He zipped up his fatigue jacket and pushed his hands deep into the side pockets. He was in civilian clothes, of course, but he had no other jacket. That and his haircut identified him as military to anyone who cared to look. Then again, the Germans never seemed to come out at night. He saw the street sign: *Donner.*

He walked three blocks to the house on the corner. He stood across the street and looked up at the third floor windows. Dark. Culp didn't think Woods was here. Woods wasn't on duty at the jail, sure, but that didn't mean he'd be home. He never seemed to be home. If he wasn't on shift, he was always in the barracks, drunk, or out getting drunk in some bar, or headed toward P street or some shit. Not here. But where was she? *Asleep, dumbass. It is four in the morning.* Ring the doorbell? Hell, did German houses even have doorbells? And what if Woods answered? Well, that was easy. He'd kill Culp. *Did the curtain move?* He'd been here before, just standing. He'd never even crossed the street. Lucky thing Woods had never seen him there. Damn sure lucky nobody had called the *polizei.* How would he explain to the German police what he was doing? For that matter, what was he doing? He didn't know. He stood there for three quarters of an hour and then headed back to the bus stop. He was an idiot. That much he knew.

CHAPTER TWELVE

15 October 1977, 1530 hours
Mannheim; Heidelberg, Germany

Jennifer Styles had made a decision. She was getting pretty good at that. That's why she was parked on Donner strasse in her little white Opel, waiting to see if Woods' wife would come out. *God! Woods' wife.* For nearly four months now, Jennifer had dickteased soldiers right down the pipe to Leavenworth, and now she'd made a decision. She'd been lonely. She'd left her only friends back at the 77th. She'd had little luck with American students, even less with German civilians. But now all that was going to end. She was gonna have Lil Woods for her own. Nothing could stop her. It was too easy, really, like shooting ducks in a barrel.

She watched Lil come out of the apartment, walk to the corner, and turn up the crossing street. Jennifer pulled around the corner going the other way so she could meet her coming head on. More natural that way. Lil was almost to the bus stop. Jennifer nosed the little Opel to the curb right in front of her. Lil looked up startled. Jennifer thought she might run, so she stuck her head out the window and called to her.

"You remember me?" When Lil didn't answer, Jennifer jumped out of the car and walked over to her. "I didn't mean to scare you."

"You didn't scare me none. I just didn't recognize you right off."

"Well, do you want a ride? I mean, where are you going? Over to BFV?"

"What's BFB?"

Jennifer laughed. "No. BF*Veeee*. Girl, you don't know what BFV is? Oh my, my, my. I don't guess Woods takes you out much, your husband, I mean. Carl."

"I know who you mean." She bit her lip. She said something else, but Jennifer was looking at the bottom lip she'd just bit. The girl's mouth was like it was always, puckered. It was like a piece of fruit, a strawberry, or a plum tilted a little sideways. She wanted to bite that same lip, right on the same place.

"I said—no. He don't take me out much. That rinky dink bowling alley. Some German place. Always with his buddies."

"Well, why don't you come with me?"

"Well, where are you going, Jennifer Styles?"

"You remember my name?" Lil laughed. Jennifer put her arm around the girl's waist and walked her to the car, settling her into passenger side. "I'm not going anyplace in particular. I just came here to get you."

Lil got back out of the car and shut the door. They stood there by the car a minute, then Lil said, "Is that true? You came here for me? You didn't just happen by? No, I don't guess you would, would you? Out here on the ass end of nowhere." They laughed again. It was easy now. "What do you want?"

"Well, baby, I know it's corny, but I want you."

Though it was not what Jennifer Styles would have chosen, they spent the rest of the day driving around Mannheim. *Jennifer Styles*, Lil had said, *let's go riding*. Okay, so they went riding. It was actually kind of fun, Lil, like a little kid, pointing out the rows of married housing in BFV, and the rows of tanks along the fence at Coleman kaserne where Jennifer hadn't wanted to go in so they just rode by. Hell, she even gotten excited about the paper mill. World's largest stink factory. *Never seen anything that big under one roof in her life,* she'd said.

They ended up in Heidelberg looking from the river walk up toward the castle. Jennifer thought Lil might have a touch of the culture shock the Army had warned them about when she had first gotten orientated to Germany. Lil's mouth was hanging open a bit and she looked kind of dumbstruck. She was worn down from pointing at everything and now was just looking around.

So Jennifer forced her hand. "You want to come over to my house? Well, my apartment really. I live right across the river."

"No you don't. Do you?"

"Yeah, right over there."

They drank off a beer passing it from one to the other, and then Jennifer dropped the empty on the floor and pulled Lil to her and put her arms around her and moved her face in close, and closer, until she could smell Lil's breath, and she breathed it in, and she waited there, just that far from those lips she wanted more than anything she could ever remember wanting, and she waited, she waited to see if Lil might just pull her that sweet last inch. And she did.

So Jennifer led her to the bed. They lay a long time kissing, exploring each other's mouths, at first really hungry, and then more slowly and softly. Lil sat up and looked at her. Then she began to undress, there on the bed, pulled off her shirt, and wiggled out of her jeans and panties. And she was naked. She unbuttoned Jennifer's blouse, and Jennifer knew Lil had understood that it was Jennifer who needed some assurance that Lil was a willing participant. And so Lil was trying to take the lead.

But now it wasn't necessary. She knew Lil was hers, even if Lil didn't know it. Jennifer got up and undressed. She went into the kitchen and got another beer. She drank some and set it by the bed. Then she got on top of Lil and began kissing her, kissing her now the way she wanted to, the way she'd been dreaming about these past lonely months. And she began to explore Lil's small body.

She moved down to get at her breasts. They weren't big, but when she sucked a nipple into her mouth, it got big and hard real quick and she could feel Lil rubbing her cunny against Jennifer's hip. She sucked back and forth until the nipples were very pink and then she headed south.

Lil responded very well. Pretty soon she was moaning real soft and bucking against Jennifer's mouth, pulling Jennifer's hair, trying climb down her throat. And then the juice started pouring out of her and she came. She didn't make much noise, just some hissing sounds, in and out, and hitting her fists on the bed.

Jennifer felt a rush of happiness. She turned over and began to rub her clit. Lil sat up and said, "Let me."

"No. Not tonight. Just wait a second." And she rubbed faster and faster, lifting her hips up. Lil would not be able to give her what she needed now. The knowing hand. Lil would require some instruction, some practice. But now Jennifer needed this, now this, and she gritted her teeth until they creaked and she came. And hugged Lil to her.

CHAPTER THIRTEEN

16 October 1977, 2330 hours
U.S. Army Area Confinement Facility
Coleman Kaserne
Mannheim, Germany

Of course, they had put Lee in solitary. What the guards called Close Confinement. The guy who ran the place, the Colonel, had told Lee that it was for his own protection, that the soldiers in the stockade might not take kindly to a deserter, somebody who'd run away from Viet Nam. Some of the prisoners and some of the guards, he explained, had served in Viet Nam. Then there was also the possibility that some of Lee's former compatriots in the Baader-Meinhof might come looking for him too. Lee didn't say much. In truth, he preferred solitary.

He'd made the little cell his home. As long as he had something to read, he could survive anything. There had been a bible on the bunk when he first got here. After his initiation by Carl Woods, he hadn't been in a very bible mood. But he'd read Micah the first night. *Do justly, love mercy, and walk humbly with thy God.* It spoke to him. The next day one of the guards took him to the library and let him take out one book. He also got to walk around on the tennis court for thirty minutes. And so he fell into a routine.

In solitary you only got two meals a day. If Woods was on duty, Lee skipped whichever meal was served then. He figured Woods was not above pissing or jacking off in his food. No matter. He'd gone without plenty of meals during his Baader-Meinhof days and even more when he was on the run. The other guards weren't bad compared to Woods. They weren't exactly friendly, but most didn't go out of their way to fuck with him.

Two meals a day and thirty minutes outside every other day. Otherwise he read or meditated. He had taught himself meditation. Close your eyes. Scrunch feet for ten seconds, relax. Flex calves ten seconds, relax. Flex thighs, relax. Stomach. Back. Shoulders, jaw, forehead. Peace. Calm. If not quite nirvana, well, as close as he was going to get. Routine. He needed it. Always had. Here routine was easy, supported by every aspect of the environment.

He just couldn't get the crying under control. Couldn't time it out. Find a regular place in the routine. It had a mind of its own. No shame in crying. The toughest guys he ever knew cried if things got bad enough. He tried to convince himself that it was mostly relief. The jail was tough living, but not as bad as life on the run in Italy after Moro. He'd had a bad first night, then things were okay for a while. For six weeks.

It was late when Woods came to Lee's cell. Lee thought he might be dreaming, but Woods hit him hard in the nose, and Lee was fully awake. Woods' sniveling cohort pulled Lee out of the bunk and held his arms behind his back. Lee was thinking that if the little bastard were in here without Woods, Lee would beat him so hard his children would feel it. Woods showed Lee a hammer, a ball peen hammer, and rapped it against Lee's ear, just enough to sting, to get his attention. His fingers pushed Lee's lips back, and Woods looked at his teeth as you would look at a horse's. Woods pulled his fingers back and showed Lee the hammer again, up close.

"If you bite me, I'll knock out each and every one of your teeth."

Lee gagged.

"You understand me?" Woods looked hard into Lee's eyes. Lee nodded.

Woods put his hand gently on Lee's shoulder and helped him down to his knees. He put his hand on Lee's head. Lee looked up. "Go ahead," Woods said. He looked at the front of Woods' pants, fatigues, with a non-regulation belt. "You take them down," Woods urged.

Lee put his hands on Woods' belt. "What you're doing is wrong," Lee said. He unzipped the pants and pulled them down.

Woods took a deep breath. The smell of death out in the hallway. A dragging footstep. Hoarse whisper. *Fear is the mother of morality.*

"I'm not afraid of anything. I'm beyond all that, all that good and evil shit."

CHAPTER FOURTEEN

17 October 1977, 1030 hours
U.S. Army Area Confinement Facility
Coleman Kaserne
Mannheim, Germany

Since he hadn't been dragged out of formation by MPs, hadn't been handcuffed in the Colonel's office, Woods was sure Lee had not dropped a dime on him. Yes, he owned the maggot. Power made flesh. Flesh made thing. Power and joy poured over him as if from a freezing waterfall, impossibly high, crystal molecules in endless return, splashing down onto him as if from the highest mountains in the Alps. Black rock in black space moving toward the speed of light, light smashing through him, every particle and wave smashing him into atoms.

But one day on Woods' shift, Lee had been in Counseling a long time. He didn't put it past that fucking Culp to wheedle the whole story out of Lee, then to run like a little girl to Stuart. Or to the Colonel. Woods waited at the gate six, near Counseling. A prisoner swabbing the main hall swung his mop ridiculously close to Woods' spit-shined boot. Ridiculous. Did the thing not know how close he was to annihilation? Woods glared at the man. The prisoner froze. He stared at Woods as he would have a snake. Woods threw his chest out. He shimmered, shone like the sun. Power radiated off him. Power struck the man like light. But then Lee came out of Counseling, and Woods had Thornton take him back to D Block. He waited to see if one of the counselors came running out looking for the Colonel. But nobody came out.

So he went in.

He hadn't been in Counseling very much. He hated the fucking counselors, the coddling ass wipes. It had gotten so he couldn't throw a prisoner in the Hole without some counselor running to the Colonel, asking for a DB hearing. Woods had stood in front of that Disciplinary Board a dozen times since Stuart took over Counseling, explaining himself in front of the likes of Dodd. And Culp, that faggot. How that little E-4 nothing squirmed his way onto the DB was beyond belief. None of the prisoners on the waiting bench stood up when he came in, and he was just about to tear them new assholes, but then he saw Culp at a corner desk in the next room talking to some maggot.

"Get on your fucking feet," he whispered close to the prisoner's ear. The prisoner ran out into the waiting area, and Culp opened his mouth to say something, but pussied out. *Fucking chicken shit.*

"Who talked to the deserter, Culp?"

"What do you want?"

"I want to know who talked to that fucking con, you shit."

Culp eased out of his chair, keeping his eyes on Woods, and carried his cup over to the coffee pot. Slowly, deliberately, he poured some coffee.

"Is there something I can help you with?" *The bastard was laughing at him.*

It was so fucking obvious that Lee hadn't told Culp anything. He was glad, but this little Culp shit was getting to him.

The top of his head felt very hot, very very hot. He had found out what he came here to find out, but now he wanted Culp to mouth off one more time and then he'd—"Motherfucker, you tell me who talked to that fucking deserter before I kick your fat ass from here to Frankfurt!"

Culp looked scared, but he just said, "Sgt. Stuart, can you come in here a moment, please." And Stuart entered, from a small office next to Counseling that Carl had never really noticed before. The unexpected sight of Stuart threw him for a loop.

Now that fucking Culp said, "Sgt. Stuart, this private *first* class has a question regarding one of our morning interviews, and he seems most anxious to have an answer, so I thought you might accommodate him." *My God, the bastard is mocking me out. Right to my face!*

And Stuart smiled at Woods. That goddamn fake ass smile, that lying politician asshole smile that says he hates your gut and would rather eat glass than look at you, but because he's better than you he can smile at you and act all polite, all fancy table manners. Stuart didn't even ask Woods what he wanted. Just took him by the arm and lead him to the door and let him out. Shut the fucking door in his face.

And then he heard it.

First Culp, then all the prisoners. Laughing. Laughing to beat the band, the fuckers. Laughing at him. And he made up his mind right there.

Culp was a dead man.

Culp worried about Lee. After Woods' visit to Counseling, Culp asked Stuart what he thought Woods was up to, but Stuart just shook his head and told him to stay away from Woods. "He's a psychopath, son. Just keep your distance, here and in the barracks. Out on the economy. You hear? The *economy*." Bur something was going on, something beyond the Red Army and half the terrorists in Europe looking to kill him, something beyond a life sentence in Leavenworth. (Stuart said that the Army would never be able to convict him of fragging his CO in Viet Nam, punishable by death. "In a worst case scenario," Stuart had told him, "they could sentence him to death on the desertion charge." But seeing the look on Culp's face, he'd quickly added that no one had been executed for desertion since 1945.) Culp also knew that whatever was going on was going on with Woods. And Culp was not going to stand for it. He was not going to stand for it because he felt something like love for Lil. *I mean for Lee. Wha? What does that mean, Lil?* He loved him like a brother. Not a romantic love, not sexual. He wasn't even attracted to men. He just admired Jessie. *I mean Lee!*

Was this what this was? Love?

Could Culp really be in love with three people he barely knew? *Two of them men?* Hell, he wasn't even sure what love was. Nothing to model feelings of love on. No one had ever loved him. That he could remember. His own parents had divorced, after having four children. His mother had turned the children, all the children, including him, over to the state. Alabama had done its best. His two younger sisters were adopted quickly because they were just four and five years old. Their names were Rose and Anne. He couldn't remember what they looked like. His little brother, John Paul, was adopted not long after. But no one ever took to Culp. So he lived in foster homes. He never caused any of his foster parents any trouble. In fact, they all seemed to like him well enough, if they noticed him. But they for sure didn't *love* him. So he really just had no idea what other people meant when they said they loved someone.

But he knew what he himself meant when he said he loved someone. He knew what his feelings were, and they weren't noble and they weren't romantic. They weren't empathetic or self-sacrificial. They boiled down to miserable, slack-jawed, weak-kneed need. A hopeless and contemptible adolescent need for someone to love him. To shelter him with love. Or friendship. Male, female, whatever. *What I want is to sleep with Lil!* He didn't want to sleep with Lee. He didn't want to sleep with Jessie. But he couldn't avoid the undeniable fact that, well, he would. He would sleep with Jessie if that's what Jessie wanted. If Jessie would love him. Or just like him. Or just let him hang around. He would let Jessie own him like a dog if that's what it would take to get under his shelter, under whatever money or influence or power that gave him the protection he needed for the life he lived. Culp would do anything, suck Jessie's dick, bend over for him. *Hell, I'd kiss his feet.* If it would get him away from the Army, from the jail, from the Fear. The lonely dread that walked with him every day like a terrible fairy tale stepmother.

Changed foster homes five times before he turned eighteen and was off the state's hands. He had worked part time during high school. Those meager saving lifted him into the local junior college for two years before they ran out. *Ran out.* The fall of Saigon had prettified the all volunteer Army's promises of a generous GI Bill. It seemed a reasonable step toward college. Culp had only learned one good thing at junior college and that was Nietzsche. The Army would be a bridge between the Culp he was and a better Culp. The Army would make him stronger. He would stride out of the Army and into a four-year college and there find—something. A place, a persona, a soul.

But that was never going to happen. The Army had shown him that he would never scale any *ubermenschlich* heights. That he would founder always, as he foundered now and had foundered then, in the foot hills, the warm water, the pleasant zephyrs. Oh, he hid among them. The Army had demonstrated with geometric logic that if Nietzsche was the Ninth, Culp was the Pastoral. Hell, he was the anti-Nietzsche, more Prufrock than Zarathustra. That was probably why he loved Lee, why he wanted to protect him. Lee was the *ubermensch*. Bomber, fugitive, killer. The awesome sum of all the awful choices he had made in his life. The existential hero. Culp was the refuse of the running, the hiding he'd done, his pitiful path of least resistance. He hadn't been creating a soul. He'd been erasing one. *No more, I swear. No more.* He was going to do one thing. *Purity of heart is to will one thing.* And he was going to do it. He was going to stop Carl Woods. He was going to step into the power vacuum left by the Death of God and forge a new self. Well, anyway. He was going to take a shot at Lil.

CHAPTER FIFTEEN

20 October 1977, 1800 hours
Donner Strasse
Mannheim; Heidelberg, Germany

Dazzling blue day. Fall was here and winter was a-coming. She wondered what the winter was going to be like. It got plenty cold in Arkansas. How much worse could it be here? And summer in Germany had been kindly nice. Lil was on a streetcar that would take her from Heidelberg to Mannheim, where she would catch a bus, if she could remember the right one, to Donner strasse. She hadn't been home in two days.

So far, Carl hadn't noticed her being gone so much. But she tried to be careful. She never spent the night with Jennifer Styles without first being sure he was on the graveyard shift.

If he's home, she thought, so be it. Her stomach fell a bit as the streetcar dropped down a hill, down the first of many, toward the river valley. Time to bring things to a head anyway. Rather have it some other way, of course. Tell him in her own time, later, at the right moment.

Jennifer Styles said there would be no right moment.

The streetcar ran right alongside a main road, and after the pretty, old, antique-looking buildings of Heidelberg had gone past, the area began to look more and more like Mannheim. Industrial. Even the places people lived in looked like office buildings. Jennifer Styles said Mannheim had been blown slap to pieces in World War Two and had had to be rebuilt right from the ground up, so there were no buildings much over thirty years old to speak of. It was obvious to Lil that whatever good taste the Germans had when they built Heidelberg had gotten blown slap to pieces too. Especially when it came to building this place back up. These new buildings looked like they had been put together with the idea of being as simple as possible and at the very same time just as ugly as possible. Keep it simple, but find a way to make it mud-ugly.

And they did.

Then again, Jennifer Styles was not completely right. Just across the street from the apartment on Donner strasse there was this bomb shelter that had to have been built before the war. It was still standing, and pretty, what little she could see of it. Of course, it was Carl what said the thing was a bomb shelter. And his mouth weren't no prayer book. Through the bushes and cedar trees somebody had let grow up around it, it looked for all the world like a church. Tall and boxy, wide stone steps leading up to the front door. What looked like marble walls was probably just concrete. It didn't have to be rebuilt. But then, that would just be common sense. If something was gonna come out standing on the other side of a war, most likely it's gonna be a bomb shelter fore it's gonna be a church, what with God not being around much lately when you needed Him and such.

To catch the bus to Donner strasse, she got off in front of BFV. She'd found out that that was Benjamin Franklin Village, a place where soldiers and their wives and families lived, like a big apartment complex, except a really really big one, with an American style grocery store and even a little Tote Sum store like back home. A convenience store deal. Except for the streetcars running by, she could be back in America. She had wondered when she first saw BFV why she and Carl weren't living there like the other married soldiers and their wives and kids. Jennifer Styles couldn't get in there, not being married and all, and so had to live "on the economy." That's what she called it. She said either Carl's enlistment wasn't long enough to qualify to get in at BFV or else he was just plain stupid.

Jennifer Styles said she thought it was the latter of the two.

There were half a dozen taxis lined up next to the streetcar stop. The German taxis were all Mercedes. Pale yellow Mercedes. But for that matter, all the garbage trucks were Mercedes too. Jennifer Styles and her sometimes rode around in these taxis. Jennifer always had plenty of money, though she also had plenty of worries about how she got it. Sometimes she hugged Lil so tight and cried. But Lil didn't want to ride up Donner strasse in a taxi, with Carl maybe looking out the window. She'd rather walk from the bus stop. No hurry anyway.

She bought a ticket from the machine at the stop, and when what she hoped was the right bus came along, she clambered on. Always through the back door to remind herself that she didn't have to show the bus driver her ticket. The habit was just too strong to break, and more than once she'd embarrassed herself by holding the ticket out to the poor driver while he tried his dead level best to ignore her. The Germans were on the honor system with the buses and streetcars, and it felt nice being trusted. She faithfully bought her ticket. Once she'd been on the bus when the Gray Ladies got on board. They checked everyone's ticket. Two soldiers boys in the back didn't have no tickets whatsoever, and the Gray Ladies snatched up their IDs, their military IDs, mind you, and gave them citations to boot. Lil had felt right sorry for them, the boys practically crying to get their IDs back. Without them they were going to be in a world of hurt back at the Army. The Gray Ladies just swept away down the aisle, their long capes flowing out behind them like a bride's train, and got off at the next stop. The boys watched the Gray Ladies through the window, and then the both of them held their heads in their hands for the rest of the ride.

Fuck 'em, Jennifer Styles had said later when Lil told her the story. Shit for brains. Deserve what they get. Besides, she said, they just went downtown the next day and paid the fine and got their IDs back. Mox nix. No biggie.

No biggie.

Lil got off at her stop in front of the bakery. She went inside and looked for something to buy. For some reason she wanted to have something in her hands when she got home. Like an excuse, *I've been to the bakery, I've been shopping* or something. There was a beautiful cheesecake under the glass counter. A lady asked her something in German so Lil pointed at the cheesecake. The woman smiled and reached into the case with a pie cutter. Lil tried to tell her she wanted the whole cake, but the woman didn't understand and came out with one piece on a square of wax paper. She looked at it and the lady a moment trying to decide what to do. Then she held up two fingers.

She carried the little box, which the lady had tied with a piece of string like the cheesecake was a present or some such, down the street toward the turn onto Donner strasse. The sky that had been so blue only an hour ago was now clouding up off to the north. It was probably raining somewhere up there. The wind whipped up a side street and blew some grit up into her eyes. She stood under the clock tower a block from her house and listened to it ring out the time. A quarter to something. She couldn't see the face of the clock from where she was standing, directly under it. She'd be able to see it from the steps of the apartment.

There was no way to tell if he was home or not. She'd lost count of his shift, didn't know when he was working and when he was off. She climbed the steps and entered the apartment. It was completely dark. The shades were down on every window. Quiet as a domino. She turned on the kitchen light and put down the cheesecake.

She didn't see him until she raised up the shutter in the living room.

Later on she'd remember it in such a way that everything was slowed way down and that the air seemed all charged up, thick and hot and white like she was inside a biscuit or floating around inside a light bulb, and that gave her a just a little edge, and she was able to duck under the first blow, a wide swinging right hand that seemed like it came from the other side of the street. But she couldn't get out from in front of the kick he followed with, and his hard-tipped boot caught her on the right shoulder, right on the ball of it, hurt like hell, and lifted her almost standing up again, just as his big old left hand came smashing into her ribs and knocked all the breath out of her, and that's when she thought he'd probably kill her.

She hadn't even fallen all the way to the floor when the right hand slammed into her jaw and smacked her head down against the uprushing floor.

She woke to the feeling of flying, and she was, and a second later she bounced off the wall and fell behind the couch. He dragged her out. The room was a mess. Her nose seemed to be running, but it was blood and it was all over the front of her shirt and his hands. She felt her nose and thought it was swoll up pretty good, but he wasn't through. He snatched her up and chucked her against the big chifferobe that belonged to the landlord. All the glass of it broke and fell down all around her and all over her. She prayed the whole thing didn't tip over on her. It weighed about a thousand pounds.

He bent over her with some kind of billy club and started hitting her on her arms and legs. She tried to crawl away, but there was glass everywhere, so she just balled up while he whaled away at her. He wasn't hitting as hard as he could. But it smarted something awful and she knew her arms and legs were going to look really bad.

He chucked the club away and dragged her by the hair through the pieces of broken glass, some of which stuck in her skin, into the bathroom. Then he started rooting around in the dirty clothes. *Oh God*, she thought, *not this, not like this. Not in here.* Now it was true she'd spent the last three nights in a row nose deep in Jennifer Styles' pussy, licking her front butt like an ice cream cone, not exactly enjoying it, then again not really hating it neither, but it by God looked pretty damn good from where she was lying right now, what with her head wedged between the pot and the tub. He found the dirty socks he was looking for, and he pulled her out and turned her over. She wouldn't let him catch her hands as she would have normally, and she tried to turn back over to face him, so he sat down full on her back and liked to have killed her because she couldn't get her breath.

He twisted her arms back real good and tied her up. Then he picked her up in his arms like he was carrying her to bed, but instead he dumped her into the bathtub, and she thought, *Uh oh*, and it hurt like fire getting dropped into the tub like that, and she was thinking *What in the world?* and then he pulled out his thing and started peeing on her. The son-of-a-bitch was peeing all over her, but mostly right on her face and on her chest so it splashed up on her face and the pee and blood were running all together. She tried to turn over, to get away from that stinking pee, but with her hands tied behind and the tub so slippery and all, her feet could find no purchase, and he was just about through anyway. He peed his last little bit right on her mouth, and she sputtered and spit, but she could taste it. She cussed him then, and as he was going out the door, he said, "Culp teach you to talk like that?" And then he was gone. She didn't know what the hell a Culp was and she didn't care. She was trying to get untied.

It took a while. At first, she couldn't sit up in the tub. Her side hurt too much. Straining to get up felt like a knife sticking her in the side. Her right ankle was as big as a grapefruit and blue as a thunderhead. When she finally got her hands free, she crawled out of the tub and hobbled to the bed where she lay down, pee and all, blood and all, and fell asleep.

When she woke, it was around noon the next day. She had stiffened up over night and made a pure mess of the bedclothes. Every inch of her body hurt. She needed to get to Jennifer Styles. But she wasn't sure she could walk to the bus stop, much less the street car stop. Then walk to her apartment. Not with this ankle. No, what she needed was Jennifer Styles coming down here to fetch her. Jennifer had a phone, but Carl and her didn't, so there was no way to call. For that matter, she didn't even know Jennifer's number. And even if they had the Information over here, it was bound to be in German. She hobbled to the bathroom and peed. The tub was smeared with dried blood. She threw up and then lay her bruised face down on the cool tile floor.

When she woke again, she thought, *Jennifer Styles*, and sat up weak and kindly sick to her stomach. She got to her feet and hopped over to the window to see how much light was left.

Down on the corner was that soldier from Coleman kaserne. She didn't know his name. To herself, she called him Chubb, whenever she thought about him. That'd be since he'd followed her home one night from Coleman. She'd seen him a couple of times since, just standing there on the corner, sometimes pacing up and down. Always when Carl was on shift. He wasn't all that fat really. There was another guy at Coleman she called Double Chubb. Worked in the snack bar. Now that boy was fat!

But Chubb here hadn't been around lately. Neither had she for that matter. She waved at him, but he wasn't looking up at the window. She threw some of her stuff into an Army green laundry bag and eased herself down the stairs sliding from step to step on her butt. It didn't take her long to get to the bottom, but from there out to the street was a booger bear. She thought she might pass out as she fumbled with the gate, but all of a sudden he was there holding the gate, and she clutched onto his arm and said, "Please, help me."

Well, she knew she looked a mess though she hadn't stopped to check the mirror on her way out. She was pretty sure her nose was flat as a hoecake, she was covered in blood, and she stunk like pee, which was really only right since she had been peed on. She'd figured that ol' Chubb had been following her around so much in the first place cause he wanted to backdoor Carl like everybody else at Coleman. *This oughta knock some of the bloom off that rose,* she thought.

It was a little chilly out and she had no shoes on and was carrying her coat. He looked at her feet, then looked again at her ankle and whistled.

"You want me to take you back inside?"

"How do you know he ain't inside waiting to do this to somebody else?"

"Saw him leave."

"Would you carry me up to Heidelberg?"

"Heidelberg? What in the world for?"

"I got a friend there. You know her, Jennifer Styles, used to work at the jail with y'all, real pretty?"

"She musta left before I got there."

"But you know who I mean."

"No."

"Sure you do. That was you following me all the way up to Heidelberg two weeks ago, and then all the way to her house. That was you what followed us to the Schnitzelbank and watched us eat supper, wasn't it? Seemed like you got a good look at her then."

"I wasn't looking at her."

"Uh huh. You taking me up to Heidelberg or not?"

"Yeah, I'm taking you to Heidelberg. How are we getting there?"

"Well, I guess we're riding the streetcar, unless you got a car or some money for a taxi."

"I've got some money. How much to taxi to Heidelberg."

"Not the foggiest. Probably a lot."

"Streetcar it is." He caught her around the waist and they headed off toward the bus stop, her hobbling and him mostly dragging and sorta carrying her.

There wasn't a bench nor nothing, so they had to just stand there. She leaned against the bus stop sign, holding her weight off her foot best she could. Chubb had wrapped her coat around her and was now just looking at her.

"Reckon they'll let me on the bus like this?" She pointed at her bloody shirt. "I don't guess I smell like no rose garden either."

"They certainly aren't in a position to complain about how a person smells," he said and smiled, and she realized he was really a sweet person, and she felt bad calling him Chubb, even if it was only in her mind, so she asked him his name.

Her mouth dropped open like an oven door.

"Culp?"

She eased her aching bones down into the water. Jennifer Styles had hot water night and day. Her bloody, peed-on clothes were in a smelly pile in the corner. The claw-footed tub was brimming full of the hottest water she could stand, and she could feel it drawing out the pain like tobacco on a wasp sting. Everywhere except her ankle, which was now swoll past all recognition. Jennifer hadn't been home when Culp half dragged, half carried her up the stairs to the apartment. She'd sent him packing as quick as she could, because she wanted to get outta them clothes, and because she had some serious thinking to do.

She tried to get her wedding ring off and couldn't. So she soaped up her finger and started pulling. One thing was for sure. She'd had a bait of Carl Woods. She'd never see him again if she could help it. If she saw him first, he'd never see her. If he saw her, she'd run. If he caught her, she'd try to cripple him. Short of that he'd have to kill her to be in the same room with her.

She'd divorce him too. First thing.

Well, if she'd noticed Culp hanging around, then Carl woulda had to too. That's what he meant. He knew she was fooling around on him and assumed it was Culp. She told Culp on the streetcar what Carl had said, about *did Culp teach you that*, and Culp said Carl'd be looking for him too, but not to worry, he would stay outta Carl's way. She truly wished that it would be so.

She felt like Jennifer Styles would probably ask her to move in here, and she supposed she would do that very thing. She reckoned she was a lesbian now, and for good reason, and there you have it, the hell with it. But even if that didn't happen,

Lil was gone. One way or another, she'd get back to Arkansas. Jennifer Styles would help her. Even if she didn't want Lil here, Jennifer cared about her and wouldn't just leave her to fend for herself.

The Army would probably send her home, but it'd be Carl that'd have to arrange something like that. No, she'd get home some other way, even if she had to walk the whole long way. Or else she'd stay here. And go home when Jennifer went home. The ring suddenly slipped over the knuckle and shot up into the air and fell on the floor and rolled right over on top of the floor drain.

Go on down, she thought.

But the sieve was too fine and the ring lay on top, halfway between hell and her finger. And it occurred to her that maybe the sieve, besides keeping you from losing your valuables down the drain, also kept whatever was down there from coming up, and the thought gave her a little chill, so she slid down into the hot hot water until her eyes were level with the grayish surface. She'd never opened her eyes under water. She wasn't going to start now.

When Jennifer turned the corner onto Molkenkurweg, the little cobblestone street where her apartment was, it was around 2130 hours, and she was surprised to see Colonel Faust standing outside the bakery eating a cookie. When he saw her coming, he brushed off his hands and came forward to shake hands with her.

"Long time no see, boss."

"I told you I wouldn't be around much."

"Something must be wrong. Are we cancelled?"

"Let's talk upstairs."

As soon as she stepped in the door, she knew Lil was back. *Why is she back so soon?* She wasn't real sure how to handle this. What would Faust say? Think? He was a pretty straight guy. He might not want a lezbo working for him. But then, if he'd really checked her out before he offered her the job—then he knew.

Faust looked around. "Is somebody else here?"

"A friend," she said evasively.

"Lil Woods?"

"I'm guessing she's in the bathroom."

"What I need to say to you, she doesn't need to hear."

Jennifer was about to suggest they go around the corner to a little cafe she liked when Lil limped out of the bathroom into the living room. When she saw the colonel, she started and the towel she was wrapped in dropped to the floor.

Jennifer gasped. "Jesus Christ in heaven. Lil, what happened?"

Lil just stood there like she was frozen or something, so Jennifer and Faust got a good look at her. She had a black eye. There was hardly a place on her from her neck to her knees that wasn't bruised. She looked like a Dalmatian, black spots on white skin. Her ankle was swollen up huge and was dark blue. She and Faust both seemed frozen too, but he moved first and picked up the towel and put it around Lil.

"You need to see a doctor," he said gently.

"No sir, I think I'm all right."

"Maybe so. I don't doubt it. But I have to tell you that I'm not going to sleep tonight unless I know for sure you are all right. Can you get dressed by yourself or do you want Jennifer to help you?"

"I can get dressed. 'Cept my shoes. I don't think I can get them on."

"Don't you worry about that. I have my car around the corner, and I'll pull it right out front. You won't have to walk far."

Lil looked at Jennifer, tears trembling in her eyes, and then hobbled off into the bedroom. Jennifer could feel her pulse beating in her temples. Colonel Faust took her by the shoulders, turned her around and walked her over to the front windows. The lights in the shops were burning bright, the sky as dark as hate itself. She was shaking.

"Don't do it," Faust said. "Don't even think about it."

"About what?"

"You know what I mean."

She turned to face him. "I won't kill him, I promise. I'll just mangle him a little. Cut his nuts off, maybe feed them to him. Beat his face to a bloody pulp. I can take that fuck, I guaran-fucking-tee it. No problem."

"No, no you can't. And I don't mean you're not able. You say you could kick his ass. Right now, I believe you. In fact, you could take him down a hundred ways, including the same way you've taken down so many so far."

"Nope. Changed my mind. I'm going to kill the fucker. I'm going to—"

Faust raised his voice. "You can't. I won't let you. You'll ruin yourself. You'll get court-martialed."

"Fuck it."

"No. I won't let you. You don't deserve the misery that would come down on you if you did. Besides I've got something important for you to do. That has to be your first priority."

"You don't get it. I have to get that bastard. Look. Do you know? Do you know about me and her?"

"Yes. Yes, of course I do. That's not the point. It's not important. You do what you have to do. We all do what we have to do. Nothing of it appears in any of my reports or evaluations. This has been one highly successful mission, and I'm scoring many points from your work. That's all I care about."

Now there were tears in Jennifer's eyes. "That's all?"

He sighed and sat down in a chair facing the high windows and the glittery German night. "No. I mean, officially, yes, but off the record, no. I've got—well, a personal investment in you too. I like you, Styles. I want the best for you, and if the best is Lil Woods, then that's what I want too. But I'm afraid I've used you. Used you terribly. As a means to an end, and not as an end in yourself." He pinched the bridge of his nose and kinda ducked his head and spoke softly, like he was talking to himself almost. "The man who said that lived a long time ago. A time very different from now. He lived in one little town all his life. The good Germans there could set clocks by him. But there are no Germans there now. It's all Russian. Now they call it Kaliningrad. Named not after the greatest mind in German philosophy, but after a petty Communist bureaucrat, a nobody, a blank slate, a man so innocuous that his great skill was being invisible enough to survive party purges." He stopped talking. He looked kinda lost and unsure, a look Jennifer had never seen on him before.

"What does all that mean?" she said.

"It means somebody else has taken an interest in our project. Someone above me in the chain of command, and now it seems we will have to do something, well—"

"Well what?"

"Something we don't know the reasons for or the consequences of. We're targeting a particular soldier. I don't know why. But you're going to go after him. See if he'll buy you some dope. Then turn it over to me."

"Same-o, same-o, sounds like to me. 'Cept for going after this one particular guy. I don't guess it's Carl Woods by any chance, huh?"

"You forget about him, Styles. I'm serious. And don't let her go home. Ever. If you decide you don't want her here, for whatever reason, call me. I'll make the arrangements to get her stateside, no problem.

"She's staying here with me."

"Fine. That's great. But forget Woods. Focus on the job right now. You've got a job to do. A soldier to bust."

"Right. What's his name?"

CHAPTER SIXTEEN

13 November 1977, 2000 hours
L'Epi d'Or
Mannheim, Germany

"Do you remember Jennifer Styles?"

Jessie and Stuart sat in L'Epi d'Or. Jessie had refused his usual table by the window for a smaller one in the back near the kitchen. It was noisy, but that's what Jessie wanted.

"Yes." Stuart was obviously savoring the memory. "She vanished like a thief in the night, as I remember. Some full bird colonel swooped down and plucked the lovely thing. Rather like the king's men seeking out and purchasing the beautiful peasant girl-child for service in the castle. But as to what really happened to her, I don't know. I assume she's in Heidelberg working some high visibility security. Fine eyewash for some general who imagines the Baader-Meinhof after him."

"Nope. Good try though. She's a narc."

"Fiddlesticks. You made that up."

"Nope. Though it does have the ring of fiction. She is working the smoothest undercover narcotics scam I believe there has ever been in the history of the CID. She's pretending to be an American student at the university in Heidelberg. She's got a car, she's got an apartment, and she's got a wardrobe."

"The hell you say."

"She picks up military types, grunts usually, in bars, makes it clear they can get laid if she can get high, and when they score her some dope, CID picks them up the next day."

"Canards." Stuart snorted. "Prevarications."

There was a pause. Jessie had more but needed to savor it.

Finally Stuart said, "And?"

"And she's got a live-in girlfriend."

"Hm." Stuart leaned back, "That jibes with the conventional wisdom from back when she was on platoon."

"But you'll never—I repeat, oh, Wise One—never imagine who it is."

"Well, let's see. Uh, Carl Wood's wife?"

"You son-of-a-bitch. Lord, isn't there anything you don't know? Who told you this?"

Stuart placed his hand over his heart. "My boy, I must have my secrets. But Styles, a narc? You certainly have scooped me there. You must tell me how you uncovered these Machiavellian machinations." He took a long drink of his wine.

Jessie was glad to oblige. "A few months ago I was—wait. Machiavellian Machinations?— "

Stuart shrugged.

"—I was slumming in Heidelberg, sitting at the bar in the Schloss—"

"Pick up bar for soldiers, I know it."

"I'm sure you do—and I'm watching her, Jennifer Styles that is, moving around the bar as if she's trying to get picked up, which by the way I'm thinking, well, that's okay, you know, to get away from the kind of guys she must be seeing at the stockade—"

"Indubitably."

"—but she's very picky, talks to a guy for a few minutes, moves on. She's the aggressor, mind you, not them. I mean, she's holding all the cards, as we know—"

"As we know."

"Anyway—she finally gets around to me. It's pretty clear at this point she is not interested in the few German guys in there. I'm thinking maybe she likes the short hair, the regular showers, whatever."

"Whatever is right."

"Will you let me tell it?"

"So tell it."

"At this point, I've found my *raison d'être*. She's the anomaly in this fairly predictable environment. So I buy her a drink—and she's drinking mineral water, by the by—and we get to talking."

Stuart opened his mouth to say something but didn't.

"Right. It's clear she doesn't remember me from the stockade. In fact, if memory serves, I was almost gone by the time she got assigned there. When I got back from Memphis, she was just coming on guard platoon. So we had passed each other—"

"'Like ships in the night'."

"Quite. She was very memorable, and I was just another dogface."

"No reason she would remember you."

"Hm. My point exactly. So imagine my surprise when she starts in with this I'm-a-foreign-exchange-student-studying-at-the-university bullshit."

"She what?"

"Yes, and I'm thinking *what the hell is going on* and before I can even assimilate this, she's moved on to, 'hey, how about getting me some hash'."

"Oh Lord."

"Uh huh, Oh Lord is right. I'm frankly dumbstruck for a moment and can't catch up, so she goes right on, like maybe some coke or some dogs or even some downers. A multitude of bells of the warning variety are clanging in my head, and so I say I'm not into any of that, and—poof—she's gone. I mean gone. Circling the bar, waiting for someone else to buy her a drink."

"And—"

"I move to a table against the wall and keep my head down. Fifteen minutes later she's breezing out the door with some shit-for-brains cannon fodder on her arm. He's practically slobbering on her tits, you understand, but I suspect they're going around the corner to Plock."

"Plock?"

"It's a block off Schlossberg. It's—well, it's the hash street. Dealers work there, with impunity, it would seem. Surely you know where I mean."

"Yes, a block off the main drag. I've been there."

"Really."

"Research, pure and simple."

"No doubt. Anyway, he leaves her at the corner and walks the block, stopping to speak to a couple of dealers until he finds what he wants—"

"Wait. You're following them?"

"Well, yes. It's night, of course, so it was easy. She's got that blond hair, you know. So, after he scores, they stroll along—holding hands for God's sake—up toward the castle, and I, you know, follow them up to the castle."

Stuart rolled his eyes.

"Here it gets a bit tricky. There not being too much traffic up there at night, I had to stay back and then I lost them. So I walked all the way up to the garden and stood there looking down at the river like some deranged nocturnal sightseer and then slowly walked back down the path. About halfway down I heard them giggling. They must have crawled off into those hedges that line the path. Then I smelled the hash burning."

"But you didn't see them."

"No. I just kept walking. But it was my intuition then that she was working some CID scam, busting soldiers on drug offenses by means that might arguably be entrapment."

"Let there be no doubt in your mind, my friend. That most certainly would constitute entrapment. But that is not a tactic much looked down upon in Army investigations. That is to say, CID might find uses for it on some occasions. But—have you considered that maybe she really just wanted some guy to buy her a block of hash? What makes you think she was out to bust people? Maybe she was using her looks to get dope, the way any woman might use her looks, her time, her attention in a bar to get drinks."

"Hold your objections, Counselor. I'm not even to the good part yet."

"Yes. I wondered when Woods' wife would come into the story."

"This past Saturday night I'm eating at Le Gourmet—"

"Ooo la la."

"—anyway, I'm just settling down to the escargot, and who should come in but Jennifer Styles and Carl Woods' wife."

"What's her name?"

"Lil. They are wearing some very expensive, if somewhat out of character evening clothes, and Lil is limping pretty badly and seems to have a black eye under her makeup. Do you suppose Styles beats her?"

Stuart frowned. "Woods would be a more likely candidate. That's one vicious son-of-a-bitch."

"And especially if he found out about Jennifer Styles."

"He's missed the boat on that one."

"I think not."

"So in they come—"

"—in they come. But on the way in, she looks at me very pointedly. Styles, that is."

"Pointedly?"

"You know, meaningfully. To make a *point*. Anyway, I'm wondering does she recognize me now, from the bar or from the stockade. No sooner does the waiter get to their table than he is scurrying over to me with a bottle of wine, compliments of 'the ladies'."

"'The ladies'?"

"Needless to say, I'm curious—"

"Needless to say."

"So I tell him to ask 'the ladies' to have dinner with me. I'm only into the appetizer. Sure enough, they come right over, Jennifer Styles beaming like the very sun shining—"

"'Her sparkling eyes in heaven a place deserve.'"

"—something like that. And Woods' wife limping behind. And, to make a long story short, dinner, talk, bullshit about them being students at the university, though it's clear neither of them are really college material. I mean, they're rubes, they're innocents abroad. Hell, Lil hardly said a word the whole meal. Bottom line was they took me back to their place and—well."

"Well what?"

"Well, what do you think?"

"You didn't prong them, did you? Tell me you didn't. You did! You crazy dog. Both of them?"

"Yes. Both of them. But I'm here to tell you, something's up."

"So to loving speak."

"Same game. We're lying there abed. Lil is asleep, having been fucked to unconsciousness by me and then Styles. Styles, by the by, is major-league in love with that one—"

"Mutual?"

"Hard to say."

"Why? Is it in Russian?"

"Ha ha. What a wit. Lil just doesn't reveal that much about herself. Maybe there's not much to reveal, I don't know. She is, after all, deep country, from the back back hills of Arkansas. Woods is damn well cosmopolitan by comparison—"

"Things are not always what they seem."

"—anyway, she's asleep. I'm wondering can I get it up one more time and do Styles again before I crash. I'm rubbing her all over, as well as I can with the three of us on that little bed, and I'm about to climb up on top of her again when she asks me can I get her some drugs."

"Uh oh."

"Yeah. Uh oh is right. Oh Lord is right. Holy crap is right."

"What did you say?"

"I said I don't take drugs—"

"Mendacity."

"—not to the point, Jack. I told her I was stationed in Mannheim, but that even I knew she could buy hash on the street not three blocks from where we were now lying. I said, 'You've been here at the university a year now, and you mean to say you don't know how to get drugs here?' She didn't know what to say to that, so she started up with the sex, except now I wasn't up for it—"

"So to speak."

Jessie sighed. "But while she's working away on me I'm thinking, *What the fuck is up?* This is not her usual routine. I watched her work the bar. She had no particular target in mind. She just asked every guy in there to score for her. But me she came after particularly. She came to a particular restaurant on a particular night looking for a particular guy—me. She didn't remember me from the Schloss. No, Stuart, she came into Le Gourmet looking for me. And why? I'm not dealing. Hell, I'm not even buying that much, just a little hash for the house. And

I'm not buying on base. I'm dealing with Germans only. Hell, I don't even think CID could know about it."

"One never knows what CID knows or doesn't know." Stuart leaned forward across the table. "Not for sure. But I get it."

"Get what?"

"It's the money."

"The money?"

"Someone at CID has gotten wind of the money."

It was not so much that a curtain lifted and showed Jessie the smoke and mirrors as much as the curtain and its supports crashed down onto the stage killing the actors, the stage hands, and the audience in the first three rows. *Of course it was the money.* It was obvious. Somebody somewhere had found out about the money. And just how much did They imagine he would be willing to pay in order to avoid a court martial, a dishonorable discharge, and jail time over a drug bust? Quite a bit, he was sure. But that was not the point. The point was to avoid the whole thing.

"I should have let the lawyer buy me a discharge when Grandfather died."

Stuart was philosophical. "Yes, my friend, you are probably right. But that is hindsight. And utterly useless because, for all practical purposes, the past is as dead as if it never happened. There is not even one thing to be done about it."

"Okay, well then, it's simple enough, right? I avoid this bitch. I don't get her any drugs, not that I would have done so anyway—"

"You might have."

"Okay, under certain circumstances I might have, but I won't. So I'm okay. Right?"

"No."

"No? What do you mean No?"

"I mean you're being naive. You don't really think the CID, if they really want to arrest someone, has to go by the book? You think they've never planted evidence, falsified reports, bribed witnesses? Of course, they have. What would it take? Styles walks down Plock street until someone sells her a block of hash. She turns it over to her boss in an evidence bag with your name on it. Next thing, you're in the stockade in pre-trial confinement."

"So what am I going to do?" Jessie said.

They were quiet for a moment. The waiter passed silently, and Jessie signaled for more wine.

"Stall her," Stuart said.

"Stall her. Why? Why stall her?"

"Because there is only one thing you can do. You've got to get out of here. You've got to get out of Mannheim, out of Germany, back to the world. Once you're there, get that hotshot lawyer on the phone. Have him get you discharged, quickly and quietly."

"How?"

"Your lawyer says something has gone wrong in the civilian world and that you need to be discharged. And that discharge needs to be expeditious. He spreads some money around and you're out. Once you're out, CID can't touch you. Here's what I'm going to do. I'll get us on the next transport flight moving prisoners stateside."

"Yes. Yes, I see. Okay. So I stall her. That's easy. I'll tell her—yes. I'll tell her that I will get her something, something that'll take some time."

"Cocaine."

"I've never heard about it being around much."

"Exactly. Tell her that's what you like, not hash or dogs or something you could get in the barracks."

"Yes. And just for good measure, I'll throw Culp into the mixture. Maybe he'll take Lil off my hands, confuse the issue, give Styles something else to think about."

Stuart sighed.

"What? What?"

CHAPTER SEVENTEEN

22 November 1977, 2200 hours
D Block
U.S. Army Area Confinement Facility
Coleman Kaserne
Mannheim, Germany

The guard slammed the gate behind Culp. Carl Woods had been on the swing shift, and Culp knew from experience the bastard wouldn't let him into close confinement, so he'd hidden out in the Counseling office until the shift change. In a few minutes the guards would call *lights out*. It was a lonely place. Each man was locked in an individual cell, six by nine feet. Bunk, toilet, sink. The toilet was less than a foot from the bunk. Prisoners were allowed one picture and one book. Lee had no picture. Culp could see the spine of a book: *Gravity's Rainbow*. He had never heard of it.

Lee was lying down facing the wall. Culp cleared his throat. Lee turned over and saw who it was, then sat up on the edge of the bunk. "How's it going?" Culp said.

Lee ran water in the sink and splashed his face. When he turned around, Culp could see the swollen jaw, the black eye. "Wha?"

"The official story is that I fell in the shower."

"Tell me what happened."

Lee shook his head.

"Tell me. You've got to tell me."

"No. I don't. What I've got to do is stay alive. What I've got to do is survive long enough to get out of here and back to the world."

"It's Carl Woods, isn't it?" Culp felt an impotent rage rising up in him. "That bastard has got to be stopped."

"And who's going to stop him? You? He'd kill you. Me? Not me. There's nothing I can do. I can't protect myself."

"Stuart can stop him. I'll tell Stuart."

"Tell him what? That I didn't really fall in the shower? How's that going to help. Word will get back to Psycho Boy, and then I'm dead."

"I don't know. Maybe he can get Woods out of D Block. Get him into a guard tower or something."

"Yeah, maybe. Or maybe not. Maybe word gets back to him and I get killed. Hey, it's all well and good for you to take the chance he won't find out, but I can't. My life is on the line. Do you get that?"

Culp got it. He could neither help nor comfort Lee. "What can I do?"

"Not get me killed would be good."

"What else?"

Lee pulled a folded piece of paper from under his pillow. "Well," he said, "there's this."

Walking back to the barracks, Culp considered the possibilities. He could tell Stuart. But what if Stuart couldn't fix it? Wha? *Stuart could fix anything, couldn't he?* Not necessarily. Stuart and Sgt. Chambers didn't really get along. So why couldn't Culp do something himself? Where was the will he was so proud of, the resolve that put him on Lil Woods' trail?

He fingered the paper in his jacket pocket. Though it's not like he accomplished anything. He bird dogged her all over Mannheim and Heidelberg, but she was always with Jennifer Styles. They'd both seen him, and he had the feeling they were laughing at him. Ha! It would take more than mere embarrassment to get rid of him. Hell, he'd been embarrassed most of his life. He believed himself willing to take an ass kicking from Woods over Lil, but Lee was right. Woods would kill both of them rather than face Army charges of assault on a prisoner. According Wilson and Williams, Woods was a murderer. What had that prisoner had on Woods that got him killed? Life was cheap in the jail. And yet Stuart had covered for Woods. If Wilson and Williams could be believed. And what did that portend exactly? Stuart. Woods.

Of course, I could just kill him myself. Woods spent many nights in the dayroom, sleeping on the couch, nobody else able to use the room. Culp had stood over him one night. The stinking drunk lay on his back with his reeking maw open, snoring, the room one big beer fart. *If I'd had a knife then, I could have slit his throat, watched him bleed out, and ended this world of shit.*

At the bottom of his duffel bag, in the back of his locker, was a pocket knife that had belonged to his grandfather. His mother had given it to him when he went into state custody. *A man carries a pocket knife,* she had told him. He decided that his mother was right. He dug out the knife and sharpened it on a stone he borrowed from a knife enthusiast down the hall. He would keep it with him at all times from now on. *A man carries a knife. And the* ubermensch *has the will to power it into his enemy's chest.*

CHAPTER EIGHTEEN

30 November 1977, 0630 hours
U.S. Army Area Confinement Facility
Coleman Kaserne
Mannheim, Germany

Everything became clear. Stuart would have to get Lee, Jessie, Culp, and himself out of the country as soon as possible. He would lead the prisoner escort detail himself. He would get Culp and Jessie on the detail and Lee would be among the prisoners. Stuart got on the phone with the Company Commander, Lieutenant Mosley, twisted his arm a bit, and had Jessie and Culp added to the next prisoner transport to the States and Lee bumped up on the roster for the same flight. He leaned back in his chair and smiled, pleased with himself. He could see a happy ending here.

Originally, Stuart had only planned to get himself and Jessie on the flight.

Then one night he found the moron Milton drunk behind the barracks. The jackass was so drunk he couldn't find the front of the building. He was crying and when he saw Stuart, he begged the sergeant to take him home. Stuart sat down next to the man, put his arm around him, and pumped him for information about First Platoon.

What Stuart discovered pushed him over the edge. Woods was beating and raping the prisoner Lee. Woods believed Culp to be screwing his wife behind his back. And was planning to beat Culp to death with his hands. At least that's what he'd bragged to his friends. It wouldn't do. Stuart tried to get Woods moved out of D Block and away from the prisoner, but no go. Yes, this was the best plan. They would all leave. Once in the States, Jessie could buy his way out of the Army, Stuart could pull some strings and get Culp and himself stationed stateside, and Lee could go to meet his fate at Ft. Leavenworth or whatever end the Army had for him. Yes, happy endings.

The door to the Counseling office burst open and the Colonel rushed in followed by, Lieutenant Mosley, Major Petty and the Sergeant Major. *Uh oh*, Stuart thought, *this cannot be good.*

Culp's stomach churned. He wondered for the thousandth time *What fresh hell is this?* It was barely light outside. The CQ had scared the living shit out of him, slamming into the room, yanking him out of the bunk, and pitching him against his locker. Wilson and Williams sat up, and, realizing that whatever was up didn't concern them, fell back into their pillows. Now he walked quickly through the cold, hunched against the wind, hands stuffed into the pockets of his fatigue jacket, terrified that he was in some kind of shit. He'd hoped to see somebody else headed to the jail in the dark, so that whatever shit was about to fall on him would be diminished, if only a little, by others made equally miserable. But as he looked over his shoulder at the empty road behind him, he knew surely that whatever was waiting for him in the jail at the top of the hill was waiting for him alone.

But, of course, he was wrong. He was always wrong. When was he not wrong? Moreover, he was an idiot. The idiot of fear.

The Idiot of Fear. He'd spent most of his life worrying. It was his defining characteristic, and most of it, most of the fear, the vast, vast continent of his fear was pointless. Phantoms of his terrorized imagination, edgy shadows of his paranoia. Stressing over nothing. Assuming the worst. The metaphysician of the absolute certainty of the notion that the universe, the entire empty unnerving universe, was waiting, trembling above him, dangling by a thread, just waiting—to fall on him. He fingered the knife in his pocket.

Stuart was waiting for him at the front gate. "Take a deep breath, old son. You're as white as a sheet. That's not a good look for a Southren boy."

"What have I done now?"

"You? You haven't done a thing. My Lord, you are one self-important son of a bitch, aren't you? No, no, relax. What we have here is, we have a hostage situation. We're working from the Counseling office. The Colonel is in there. Major Petty, the sergeant major. And Dodd is coming in."

"Is it Lee?"

"Lee. No. He's locked up tight in D Block. Don't worry about him. We are all set to go. Lee, Jessie, you, me, we're all on the next flight out. No, I'm afraid, my friend, that our current situation may center on Travis."

"Travis? Travis? Wait, you mean the company clerk Travis? What the—?"

"We had him on the phone for a minute. What he's saying is that he is being held hostage in the Chaplain's office by some prisoners from B Block. And, uh, Ackermann is there too, you know, the chaplain's assistant."

"Aw no. Not him. He'll freak out. What am I saying? He's already freaked, I guarantee you. Jack, you gotta do something."

"We're trying to get them on the phone again, but they're not answering. The Colonel wants you to try to talk to them."

"Me." Culp felt dizzy.

"Hostage negotiation 101, old son. Easy stuff. Just get them on the phone, get them talking. Keep them talking. Get them negotiating for something, even if it's just pizza. Oh, and here's something I bet you didn't know."

"Add it to the world of shit I don't know."

"You're a member of the hostage negotiation team."

"Don't fuck with me, Jack, I'm begging you. I'm not up for this."

The Counseling Office was buzzing. The Colonel was on the phone at Dodd's desk. Major Petty sat across from him. The Sergeant Major passed Stuart and Culp going out. "They've got *me* getting coffee, for God's sake. I'll be in my office, Jack."

"Roger that. I'll get some coffee in here double quick."

"If they notice I'm gone, give 'em some story, would you?"

"A-fucking-ffirmative, Top."

The big man lumbered through the door and headed for the Front Office. Stuart shut the door behind him and turned to Culp. "Don't say anything unless the Colonel asks you something. Even then, don't answer him right away. Give me a chance to jump in if I can."

"No problem. I got nothing to say."

Culp walked over to the window. He could see the window of the Chaplain's office across the yard, but he couldn't see anybody in there. The Colonel jumped to his feet and yelled into the phone.

"No, god damn it! Who said to call the MPs? Did I tell you to call the MPs? Since when are you running this goddamn facility?" The Colonel's face was red all the way up and into his flat top.

"Who's he talking to?" Culp was trying to hide behind Stuart.

Stuart leaned toward Culp and whispered into his ear, "I think it's the company commander. Lieutenant Mosley just may have overstepped his authority and brought the MPs into the mix."

"Why the hell *wouldn't* we get them involved?" Culp whispered.

Why not indeed? Stuart wondered. *What is the Colonel up to?*

The door slammed open and Sgt. Taggart reported to the Colonel. "Well?" the Colonel stared the man down.

"He's on his way, sir." Sgt. Taggart said.

The Colonel sat down and put his head in his hands. In a few minutes Sergeant Holliday came in and reported to the Colonel, snapping to attention and saluting. Stuart considered Holliday the only sane platoon sergeant at the jail. The Colonel returned a tired salute and said, "Report."

"We just did a full count. Two prisoners are missing from B Block. Pitts and Bradford. They have to be in the Chaplain's office."

"How did they get control of the office?" The Colonel seemed to be speaking to the top of the desk.

"Sir, I can only surmise they had some kind of a weapon, a shank probably, a sharpened spoon or broom handle, I'm guessing." Sergeant Holliday fidgeted. *What's going on here,* Stuart wondered. *Does Holliday know something?*

Holliday coughed. "Sir."

"Sergeant, I want you to put a squad of men just downstairs from the Chaplain's office. Riot gear, shields, M-16s."

Stuart cleared his throat.

"Sir." Sergeant Holliday clearly had something on his mind.

"Holliday. Sergeant Holliday. I want you out front. I need you out front. As soon as you have the squad in place, I want you to get out to the front gate. I want you to get rid of the MPs that are on their way here now. They cannot come inside the jail. They cannot know what's going on here. I'm not sure what Mosley has told them. Whatever it is, you're going to deny it. Tell them there's no hostage situation. Tell them we have everything under control here. Tell them whatever you need to tell them to get them the hell out of here. I don't care if they have a full bird colonel out there. Get rid of them."

Stuart was confused. *Why isn't he sending me out there? I've dealt with those guys a hundred times.*

Sgt. Holliday said, "Sir, I'm the platoon sergeant on duty here. I'm—"

"Shift change in ten minutes. Sergeant Chambers and First Platoon will be coming in any minute. I'll be sending your men out, except for the assault squad. I don't expect to have to use them, but I want them in place now. Just get them in place and then get out to the front gate."

Holliday clearly had something to say. *Why doesn't he just say it?* Stuart thought. And then he understood. *He wants to know how the company clerk got inside the Chaplain's office in the first place. Hell, he wants to know how Travis got inside the jail at all.*

Holliday hesitated a second and then left. The Colonel looked at Stuart and Culp. "Specialist Culp. Get on the phone, start dialing the Chaplain's office. I want you to make contact. Ring it until somebody answers. I don't care how long it takes." He looked at Culp as if for the first time. "You do know what to do, right?"

Culp opened his mouth, but Stuart answered. "Sir, Spec Four Culp is our most capable man. He's well trained in hostage negotiation techniques. If anyone can get them to come out, it is he."

"'It is he.' Hm. Well, I hope you're right, Sergeant. If not, we'll have to storm the place. And I'm afraid the guards on the assault team may not be as well trained in keeping hostages alive as 'he' is in his job." The Colonel looked tired. Culp thought he looked scared, but that couldn't be right.

Stuart led Culp to Puckett's desk in the corner of the room. Culp sat and stared at the phone for a long moment before Stuart came back and wrote the four digit number for the extension in the Chaplain's office on the blotter. He handed Culp the receiver and pointed. The numbers swam in his vision.

What if somebody answered? What was he supposed to say? *Keep them talking,* Stuart had said. *Ask them if they need food or cigarettes. Trade them for hostages or other concessions.* Culp dialed the first number. Everything around him seemed to speed up and blur. He felt like a pocket of stillness in the center of a tornado. He tried to dial the second number. Which time, he wondered, was the real time? Was he slowed down or had everything else speeded up? Maybe time was passing more quickly for him because he was moving more slowly. And while he was growing older and older, sitting in stasis, immobile, those around him, moving closer to the speed of light were not aging, time was not moving as fast. Stuart, passing on the way to get the coffee he'd told the sergeant major he'd take care of, slapped him on the side of the head.

The phone system, like the stockade itself, was left over from the Third Reich. Most of the time when you dialed a number, you got a fast busy signal that meant no connection. He dialed the number a dozen times before it actually rang. Ten rings and still no answer. Twenty-five, nothing. He laid the receiver on his shoulder and rummaged in Puckett's desk drawer. Wrigley's gum wrappers, paper clips, rubber bands, eraser crumbs, pencil stubs, tweezers, nail clippers, folded paper footballs. Pen knife, hard candy, pens, tacks, loose staples. Culp shut the drawer and pulled a paperback novel out of Puckett's inbox. *The Looking Glass War.* John Le Carré. Culp read the back cover. Spy stuff.

He'd left his *Portable Nietzsche* back at the barracks. He heard a buzzing, a small, scratchy voice. Somebody had answered the phone.

"Who is this?" Culp said.

"Who the fuck are you?" Culp recognized the company clerk's voice. Travis was a short, wiry black man with tiny gold-rimmed glasses, like something out of the sixties. And like a lot of guys still around after Viet Nam, guys who had been drafted, Travis affected a militant attitude toward the Army. Back in the world he might have been a Black Panther.

"It's Culp."

"What the—Cup? Holy Mother of Shit. What the fuck are you calling here for? Don't you know what's going on? I will kill these motherfuckers. Do you hear me?"

"I hear you, Travis. What's all this about?"

"You poor fat cumbubble. I gotta go."

"Wait. Uh, do you want some pizza?"

"Say what?"

"Or some cigarettes?"

"Cigarettes?"

"Yeah, I can get you a whole carton. Um, if you let one of the hostages go."

"Where are you, Cup?"

The Colonel and the others had begun to gather around Culp when they realized that he was actually talking to somebody in the Chaplain's office. The Colonel nudged Culp's shoulder. "Who is it? Who're you talking to?"

Culp covered the mouthpiece. "It's Travis. I think it's him calling the shots. He said *he'd* kill somebody." The Colonel glanced at Stuart. And, for the first time, Stuart felt things slipping away from him. He could not get a grip on the situation.

"Well, goddamn, Cup. What are you supposed to be? The mouthpiece for the Man? They put you up? They put it all on your shoulders? Have mercy, Lord."

"What are their demands?" the Colonel asked.

"Who's 'they' you're talking about?" Culp asked.

"Ask them what they want, Specialist."

"Sure. I mean, yes sir, Colonel." Into the phone, "Travis, what do you want, man? What are you doing this for?"

"Okay. I guess it's you, Cup. Fine. Here's what I want. I want Stuart up here in five minutes. I want him alone. And unarmed. In fact, send him in his underwear. I don't want him hiding a gun somewhere."

"You're kidding, right? You want Stuart in his underwear."

Stuart stood up straight and looked at the Colonel. The Colonel met his gaze, but Stuart didn't like the look in his eyes. *This isn't right.* The Colonel lifted his chin to indicate Stuart should strip. Stuart held the Colonel's gaze a second longer and then started pulling out his shirt tail.

Sergeant Chambers stood before First Platoon in the parking lot of the stockade. The squad leaders reported their sick call numbers and fell back into formation. Chambers called out four names, then ordered the platoon to their posts and dismissed the formation. He called the four men aside. He told them to put on their riot gear, to draw weapons (M-16s and .45s), and to relieve the complement of Second Platoon stationed at the foot of the stairs to the Chaplain's office. He put Carl Woods in charge of the detachment.

Stuart strode down the hall in his skivvies, his t-shirt, and his low quarters and black socks. He had attached his stockade ID badge to the waistband of his skivvies. Despite his ridiculous appearance, he walked with the dignity of a man going to meet the President of the United States. Not one guard between the Counseling office and the back stairs laughed, snickered, smiled, or even met his eyes as he passed. They unlocked gates for him and stood aside as if nothing in the world was out of the ordinary, as if Sgt. Stuart walking down the hall in his underwear was the most natural thing in the world. Of course, to Stuart everything was wrong. *What was the Colonel doing? Why not spend more time negotiating? Why cave to their first demand? And why cave at all when it so obviously put his life in danger?*

Reaching the bottom of the stairs, he beckoned the squad leader and told him that under only the most extreme of circumstances should they even take the safeties off on their rifles. "You're Diaz, aren't you?" The squad leader nodded. "Look, Diaz, I have to go in there. I'm under orders to go in there. And I don't want to go. Do you understand that?" Diaz shook his head, then nodded vigorously. *He understood. He wouldn't want to go in either.* "Do not shoot me. Do not shoot Ackerman." Puzzled look. "The chaplain's assistant." Diaz nodded. "Okay," Stuart said. "I'm going up." He turned to the rest of the squad. "Weapons on safety, boys." He flashed a smile. Smiling Jack.

Five minutes later Carl Woods and three border-line morons from First Platoon relieved Diaz and his men.

Stuart stopped at the top of the stairs. He took a long look at the door. He had been up here a dozen times in the last six months, never really noticed the door. It needed painting. He'd see about it tomorrow. Hand-carved sign—*Chaplain's Office*—made by prisoners in the woodshop. It could use a little touch up too. He closed his eyes, took a deep breath—for a second he saw his mother's face from the picture he kept in a frame in his room—and knocked. He probably should have stood to the side in case a round came smashing through the door in response. A moment later Ackermann opened it and smiled and stepped back for Stuart to enter. Travis was sitting at the Chaplain's desk. The two prisoners were sitting on a low couch, wringing their hands and crying. *Yelling, guns flashing, threats, gut-wrenching fear, yeah, okay, bad enough, but this is worse. I don't know why, but this is much worse.* He thought of Cassandra: *It's this house— it fumes with stench and spilth of blood.*

Sitting at the Chaplain's desk, a .45 in his hand, feet propped on the typewriter, Travis looked for all the world like a student radical sitting in the president's office at Columbia University back in '68. Different expressions raced back and forth across his face. Then he put his feet and floor and dropped the pistol. He laid his head on the desk and began to cry. Stuart looked at Ackermann, who shrugged and got himself a sandwich and sat on the couch next to the terrified prisoners. He offered half, but they waved it off.

Stuart sat in the chair in front the desk. "Travis, what in the hell is going on here? For the love of God, man, have you taken Ackermann hostage? What am I saying? What, what is it that's—" He threw up his hands and slumped in the chair.

Woods removed the clip from his M-16, knocked it against his helmet, and slammed it back into place. "Okay, listen up you numbnuts. I'm going around to C Block and see if I can get a sightline into the window in the Chaplain's office. If I can get a shot, you'll hear it. If that happens, you go through that door and kill anything that moves. Try not to kill the chaplain's assistant if you can help it."

Thornton was trembling. He said, "I think Sgt. Stuart may be in there."

"Stuart? What're you talking about? Stuart's not in there, you shit-for-brains. It's that shitbird from the company office, what's his name, Travis. He's in it with the prisoners. *He's in it with them.* Do you hear me? He's some kind of Black Panther radical out to destroy the great institutions of the United States. Starting with the Army apparently. Well, he's not going to get away with it." Woods started down the hall, then turned around. "You hear my shot you go in quick, you understand?" Thornton nodded, but he did not look happy about it.

Nobody was moving in the jail. Nobody was going to chow or to the library. Nobody was trying to call their lawyers or see the Colonel. The prisoners were on lockdown until the situation was resolved. So there was no one to see Woods walking through the jail in full riot gear with a loaded M-16. Stomping into C Block like some Norse warrior, he ordered the guards to move all the prisoners to the other end of the block, away from the windows facing the yard. He found a bay with windows that looked straight across to the Chaplain's office. He turned a bunk on its side and pulled it up close to the window and propped his rifle on the window sill. He took off his belt and used it to secure the weapon to one of the bars on the window. Then he sighted in on the window across from him and settled down to wait for some future corpse to step into his line of fire.

"You've got to tell me what's going on, Travis." Stuart was pacing back and forth, sawing the air with his hands. He turned and looked at Ackermann who was still eating a sandwich and who looked away and started whispering to the prisoners. "It's okay," he was saying. "Everything is going to be okay."

One of the prisoners—Stuart didn't recognize either of them—clasped his hands as if in prayer and said, "We didn't have nothing to do with this, Sergeant. We's just told to report to the Chaplain's office and then, then," and he broke down crying. Ackermann moved over on the couch and put his arm around the man, but wouldn't look at Stuart. Travis finally raised his head from the desk.

"He's right, Stuart. I mean, Sergeant Stuart." Travis' eyes were red and bleary.

"It's all right, son. Just tell me what's going on here. I can't fix it if I don't know what it is."

"I know you're the fixer, sir. I mean, Sergeant. But this is too fucked to be fixed." Travis got up and came around the desk. "Okay, here it is."

Ackermann said, "Travis. You're not supposed to tell him. We're under orders."

Travis said, "Shut up, man. Those orders are going to get us killed. Or court-martialed. Or something anyway. Oh God, anyway you look at it, we're fucked here."

"No," Ackermann said, rising from the couch and coming to face Travis. He put his hands on the other man's shoulders and said, "We've got to trust the Colonel."

"The Colonel?" Stuart said. "What are you talking about?"

"The Colonel, he—" Travis began.

"Travis, don't. Please—"

"Shut up!" Stuart pushed Ackermann away and faced Travis. "Go on. What about the Colonel?"

"So about a week ago the Colonel calls me into his office. Hell, I'd never even been in the jail before. He tells me he wants to run an exercise, a readiness thing about hostage situations, and he wants me to come up here and pretend to be part of some hostage situation so that the guards and the officers can get some experience with all that, and he'll put a commendation in my file and I'll get some leave time and maybe even a transfer back to the world. I didn't think it through. I was just trying to do what I was told and then—"

"Wait, wait. Are you saying that this is an exercise? Is that what you're saying? This is all fake? There's no hostage situation at all?" Stuart's stomach fell. *What could the endgame here possibly be?*

One of the prisoners said, "We didn't take nobody hostage. Lord help me, Sergeant, I'm just here on a hash possession charge. I'm sposed to go to Ft. Riley. I'm not even getting discharged. I'm sposed to come back into the Army after I do my time—"

"Hush," Stuart said. He was trying to think. *What is the Colonel up to?* Travis was pacing up and down, getting more and more agitated. He stopped and pointed his finger at Stuart. Then there was a quiet tinkle of glass as the round passed through the window. And then Travis' head exploded, splattering Stuart's face with blood and bone. Travis' body slammed against the far wall, and Stuart staggered back, trying to wipe his eyes. Four rounds came splintering through the door. Three of them hit Stuart in the chest, killing him instantly and sprawling him into the file cabinets. The guards smashed through the door, and seeing the prisoners standing in front of Ackermann, opened fire on them on full automatic, killing the prisoners and, incidentally, Ackermann.

The team stood in the middle of the carnage breathing hard.

"Uh oh," said Thornton. "I think we killed the chaplain's assistant."

"And then some," said one of the other men.

They stood openmouthed trying to take in the destruction they had wreaked, when Woods came running in. He slipped in the blood which now covered the entire floor and fell hard on his shoulder.

"God damn it! Get me up." When Thornton got him to his feet, Wood drew back and hit him square in the mouth, knocking him down onto the bloody floor. "What the fuck have you done? You killed the chaplain's assistant. And, oh my God, you've killed Stuart. You killed Stuart, you stupid fucking idiots. Did you even look before you fired?"

"We didn't shoot him. We didn't see him. We shot through the door. That must have been it. He was behind the door when we shot. He shouldn't have been standing there!"

Thornton was babbling, slipping in the blood, trying to get up. Nobody offered him a hand.

Woods went around the desk, found the pistol, and placed it in Travis' hand. "He was about to shoot Stuart, so I took the shot. You guys panicked and shot through the door. It's going to be okay. Stuart and Ackermann were just in the wrong place at the wrong time. Tough luck." He left the room and the others followed him, trusting him to pull them out of the world of shit he'd led them into.

"Colonel, I appreciate your position, I surely do," Captain Montgomery said. Montgomery was the CO of the 53rd MP Company at Coleman kaserne. "Though I'm not sure, with all due respect, Colonel, that I could *paraphrase* your position."

"Just what is that supposed to mean, Captain? I'm assuming you can see the rank on my collar. I'm a lieutenant colonel. I outrank you. This is my jail. I outrank everybody in it. And I'm telling you to withdraw."

"When I say that I couldn't 'paraphrase your position' what I mean is that I don't understand your position."

"Listen up, Captain. When it comes to orders, it's not paramount that you understand. Only that you comply. Only that you take your men, you get in your jeeps and you drive back to your own area of operation" The Colonel was yelling and leaning into Montgomery, who held his ground.

Montgomery wiped a speck of spit from near the corner of his eye, then took off his cap and dropped it at the Colonel's feet. The Colonel looked at the cap. He looked up into the captain's face openmouthed.

"Then let me see if I can paraphrase *my* position for you, Colonel. The commanding officer of the 77th MP Detachment called my first sergeant and told him there was a hostage situation at the stockade. Now I don't know what my position here is exactly. I'm not sure if your men or my men are supposed to respond, but that is all about to be straightened out because there's a *full bird* colonel on his way here from Drexel kaserne right this minute. And when he gets here, he can order me to stand down or he can order me to knock you out of the way and go into that jail and free the hostages, but whatever he orders I will do. And I will wait right here for him to arrive."

The Colonel made some sputtering sounds, but nothing intelligible came out. He raised his hand as if he might strike the captain, who did not move, but just then a soldier—the sergeant major!—came running out of the front gate. He whispered something in the Colonel's ear that drained every speck of color out of the Colonel's face. Montgomery thought the Colonel would pass out, but instead he turned and walked back into the jail. The Colonel was trembling, but he held his head high.

CHAPTER NINETEEN

5 December 1977
Frankfurt-Hahn Airport
Frankfurt, Germany

Something was burning. Somewhere. Smelled like an electrical wire had shorted out in the walls. Culp sniffed at the air like a dog and looked around the airport waiting area. It was the exact same area he'd come through when he arrived in country. A shabby green linoleum floored, green-walled room with huge floor-to-ceiling windows, one facing the baggage area and one the tarmac. The prisoners were lined along one of the walls. They were all handcuffed, one to the next, so they looked a little like a bunch of children holding hands, playing Red Rover or something. Most of them were talking quietly, joking and laughing, glad to be out of the jail, away from the guards, almost as if they were getting released when they got to the world, and not just going to a different jail. Leavenworth for most of them, Ft. Riley for a few. Culp couldn't believe either would be an improvement over the stockade for any of them, except for Lee.

Lee was among the prisoners, of course. Standing quietly, looking at the ground, his uniform for traveling a shamrock-colored jumpsuit. All the prisoners were wearing them, the bright emerald hue making them stand out from the soldiers traveling on the same plane. *If only they each had a red carnation on their lapels,* Culp thought, *they could pass as Christmas ornaments.* Culp tried to catch Lee's eye, but Lee never looked up. On the other hand, Carl Woods couldn't take his eyes off Jessie and him. *How the fuck had he gotten transport duty for this trip?*

Jessie was talking nonstop. Probably nervous about the flight. Culp's bowels were water. He hated flying. At least he hated thirteen- and fourteen-hour long flights. Especially military flights. He would puke almost for sure. Sometime, now or later. On the plane or off. Here or there. He was sweating, even though it was freezing outside, and not much better inside.

"'Come, come thou bleak December wind, And blow the dry leaves from the tree! Flash, like a Love—something, something, and take a Life that wearies me.' Cheer up, Culp, old son, old Byronic hero, old Overman of the Oversoul. Half a day now and we'll turn your orphan over to the federal authorities."

"Don't be so dramatic. You're making me " Culp covered his mouth and leaned forward holding his stomach.

"Not I. I am not responsible for your dyspepsia. You are the Nietzsche of the Air Age. You have vomited within fifteen minutes of every mention of this flight for three days. You have sat the toilet for hours at a time with diarrhea, the result of merely considering what clothes to pack."

"Jack's dead. The Colonel's being court-martialed. And you're out of your mind and making me nauseated. So will you please be quiet? Please?"

"And how the hell does Woods rate a flight home after killing Stuart?"

"He didn't kill Stuart. He killed Travis, who he thought was a terrorist. Under orders."

"Isn't that what Eichmann said? Hey, does Lee look bad to you?" Jessie nodded toward the line of the line of prisoners. Lee looked like Culp felt. He was leaning against the wall, mouth slack, face gray.

"Airsick," Culp said, gagging on the second syllable.

"You're projecting, Sigmund. He looks really bad."

At that moment one of the prisoners, an tall guy with a red crew cut and prominent Adam's apple, broke into song. He sang "O Holy Night" in a strong clear baritone, worlds apart from the nasal South Carolina drawl Culp knew was his speaking voice. Culp thought, *I'm taking Gomer Pyle to Ft. Leavenworth.* Sgt. Chambers, who was leading the escort group, stepped down the line to where Gomer urged the world to "fall on your knees." It was all so incongruous. Sgt. Chamber's voice got louder and louder. The prisoner sang louder and louder. Sgt. Chambers couldn't get the singer to hear him. The prisoner's eyes were shut fast in rapt concentration. The prisoners up and down the line were smiling and laughing, and Jessie was laughing, and Culp forgot his stomach for a moment. The prisoner was singing. Chambers was yelling in his face. Lee looked up and met Culp's eyes. Laughter rang throughout the waiting area. Sgt. Chambers touched his chest. Jessie sang softly. Others picked it up and sang along as well. Chambers was brushing something off his shirt, a spreading wet spot. Carl Woods unholstered his pistol. Singers were gesturing wildly. Chambers fell to his knees, another wet spot on his chest. Gomer Pyle sang, "O night divine." Woods locked a clip into the pistol. Culp wondered if he would really fire it here. Chambers toppled backward. Jessie was up and heading for Chambers when Woods fired a round into him. Everyone got down. The noise of the pistol in the enclosed area deafening. Soldiers, families, prisoners, all now on the floor, scrambled among each other trying to get even lower. Culp didn't see Jessie fall because he was already on the floor when Jessie got up. Culp had dived for cover as soon as he saw the clip disappear into Woods' gun. He was under the bench and others were trying to get under there with him. But past the wriggling bodies he could see Woods searching the chaos for him. Woods turned quickly and started firing at the men on the floor over where the prisoners were. Where the other guards were trying to load *their* weapons. None of them got a shot off. Woods killed them all. His own people. His brother guards.

Woods flicked out another emptied clip and surveyed the room. *Looking for me.* Culp tried to hide his face. Out of nowhere a man in a pilot's uniform thumped Woods on the back of the head with a little stick, and Woods went down hard. *A leather sap, that's what it's called,* Culp thought. Another man also dressed like a pilot helped the man with the sap search among the men shot on the floor. They pulled up Lee and cut his handcuffs away. *He's escaping! He's escaping and I'm an accomplice.* Just then the customs MPs smashed in through the glass windows but held their fire, trying to figure out what was what. One of the pilots fired several rounds toward the MPs, and he was shot dead. The other pilot turned quickly and shot Lee in the stomach and in the face, and then four or five bullets from the one MP left standing knocked him over, and he shivered and died. Culp pushed his way out from under the bench and went to look for Jessie.

Jessie had been thrown across the slick linoleum and come to rest on his side, facing the wall. Culp couldn't see his face and he might have been sleeping but for the canteen-sized hole in his back. Exit wound. He grasped Jessie's shoulder to turn him over when a boot smashed into his short rib and knocked the breath out of him.

He was staring up into the contorted face of Woods, who held his forty-five—Culp could see the caliber clearly at this range—in both hands directly above Culp's face. "I'm the lightning outta the dark cloud, man." Culp stared. A strand of drool stretched downward from the corner of Wood's mouth. "You gotta have a good memory to keep all the promises you make, Culp."

Then Culp knew he was going to die, knew it in a way he hadn't known in the excitement of the gunfire. The Fear began to claw its way out his guts.

The first round knocked Woods' left arm off. It flew through the air turning over and over until it smacked against a wall across the room. A torrent of blood splashed to the floor and Woods fell on Culp. The gun was still in the hand that was no longer Woods'. They were nose to nose now. "Did God fuck up when he made us, Culp? Or did we fuck up—" Then a torrent of blood poured from his mouth onto Culp's chest and he died.

Culp wiggled out from under the dead man. Woods' blood covered the front of Culp's Class A uniform. All around him the din of voices, dying, crying in fear or pain. All around him dead men. Chambers was sprawled on his back, eyes wide, mouth open, one hand clutched to his chest, two small holes in his sternum. The last MP, a huge black man, his face fixed in a grimace of rage or fear, was high stepping through the writhing bodies, advancing on Culp with his M-16 pointed at Culp's belly. He looked like a giant.

Culp raised his hands over his head.

"Put your hands down, Cup." He walked past Culp to where Woods' arm lay on the floor.

"Who are you? How do you know me? You saved my life."

"And I had to kill a man to do it too."

"Wait. I know you."

"I didn't wanna kill no man. I didn't come into this Army to kill no man. I just wanted to—get out, get away—I wanted—to—"

"What's your name?"

The big man turned his face toward Culp and Culp could see he was crying. His name tag said "Thompson." Culp remembered. From the 42nd MPs.

Customs!

"You saved my life, man."

"What's it profit me to save your life if I—" Thompson paused. "I bought you your first German woman too. That don't make me your daddy." He looked around at the utter chaos of the room. "What in the hell is going on here?" And then he turned and walked away toward the broken glass wall, just as a whole squad of MPs arrived, and he passed through them and was gone.

CHAPTER TWENTY

25 December 1977
Heidelberg, Germany

Winter Solstice. Christmas Day. Yuletide. The sky was startlingly blue. Culp was in jeans and his field jacket, standing on a brick street in Heidelberg.

It was his first time out in a while. He'd been confined to the barracks for three weeks. Not that he'd been charged with anything or that anybody thought he'd done anything wrong, but the Army was having trouble straightening things out—who killed who, who the guys in pilots' uniforms were, was Lee trying to escape? Was Woods a hero or a criminal? CID officers interviewed Culp there in his room six times. His story was always the same. Woods had killed Jessie, Woods had tried to kill him, but an MP shot Woods first. Why, they asked him, had Woods killed Jessie. He told them he didn't know, and in retrospect he supposed that was true. The motherfucker was crazy, he had wanted to say. Every time they came he expected them to ask if he knew Thompson, but they didn't. Every time they came he expected them to show him the note he smuggled out of the jail for Lee. But they didn't.

He tried to ask them some questions, about Thompson without mentioning him by name, about Lee and the men who killed him. But, of course, they didn't tell him anything. Eventually they told him he could leave the barracks, go back to work, resume his life.

Jessie, Stuart, Lee. All dead.

What life?

Instead of going back to work though, he took some leave time. He didn't really have any money to go anywhere. What he wanted to do was catch up with Lil. So he took his sleeping bag and went to Heidelberg. Two days now he'd hung around outside that bakery over which Jennifer Styles had lived, and two nights now he'd slept in the bushes up at the castle, drinking cheap white wine and watching the river creep by, the lights winking on the bridge and in the houses beyond.

This morning he had pommes frites and a lemony German coke for breakfast. He'd gotten them through a window that looked out onto the street from someone's kitchen. Inside, children laughing, a TV blaring something in German, ordinary life, except they sold food through a window in their house.

He had a couple more days leave left. But he was going back today if he didn't find her.

The door to the apartment opened and a man in uniform emerged. He locked the door and came down the stairs slowly, tossing the keys from hand to hand. He saw Culp and walked over to him.

"She's gone, Culp."

The man was a full-bird colonel.

The colonel looked up at the sky and shrugged. "You can never know what's going to happen, Culp. 'The sky flashes, the great sea yearns. We ourselves—'"

"How do you know my name?"

"We ourselves, Culp, flash and yearn. But our women are gone, back to the world, together. That's me being optimistic, being positive, as if they were ever ours. You never really got in the game, did you?"

Culp didn't get it.

"No. It wasn't in the cards for you. Or her. Husband so bad, she'd take a lesbian in exchange. Probably not enough vocabulary to know the word 'lesbian'. Maybe not even enough experience to know there were such people. Husband gone psychotic, shot down like a dog. Causing the deaths of a dozen more-or-less innocents."

"I think this might all be my fault," Culp said.

"Really?" The colonel seemed to consider the idea.

"No," he finally said. "In some sense, it's mine. I lost control of the operation, too eager to please, too proud of what we'd done. I didn't see what They were up to, and we made him run."

Him, Culp thought, *who's him? Woods?*

"Not directly caused, you see. I stamp my foot here—" and he stamped the brick street "—and a man falls off his bicycle in Peking. You understand? Butterfly wings and hurricanes?"

Culp nodded, but he was lost.

"But no, not you. You tried to help, right? Whatever your motive." And he turned away and walked up the street. Culp watched him go.

Then he stopped and turned around.

"But then again, I don't know everything. Do I?"

Culp had no intention of telling him everything.

The colonel ducked his head and lifted a hand in goodbye. Then he was gone, turned a corner out of sight. Culp felt a thousand light years from home.

ABOUT THE AUTHOR

John Calvin Hughes lives and works in Florida. He is the author of *The Novels and Short Stories of Frederick Barthelme*, a critical study, and *The Shape of Our Luck*, a poetry chapbook. *The Twilight of the Lesser Gods* is his first novel.

Made in the USA
Charleston, SC
05 April 2012